The Earth-Shaker

Recent books by Lin Carter:

HUROK OF THE STONE AGE
WEIRD TALES #3 (editor)
DARYA OF THE BRONZE AGE
MYSTERIES OF THE WORM (editor)
CONAN THE BARBARIAN (with L. Sprague de Camp)
FLASHING SWORDS! #5 (editor)
KELLORY
ERIC OF ZANTHODON
WEIRD TALES #4 (editor)
THE EARTH-SHAKER

Zarkon,
LORD OF THE UNKNOWN,
In
The
Earth-Shaker

A CASE FROM THE FILES OF OMEGA,

AS TOLD TO

LIN CARTER

DOUBLEDAY & COMPANY, INC.

GARDEN CITY, NEW YORK

1982

All the characters in this book
are fictitious, and any resemblance
to actual persons, living or dead,
is purely coincidental.

Library of Congress Cataloging in Publication Data

Carter, Lin.
Zarkon, Lord of the Unknown, In The earth-shaker.

I. Title.   II. Title: Earth-shaker.
PS3553.A7823Z23   813'.54
ISBN: 0-385-12477-5   AACR2
Library of Congress Catalog Card Number 76-42320

First Edition

For Paul Ernst,
creator of the Avenger,
and for Captain George
and all my friends
in the Vast Whizzbang Organization.

Contents

x   *Contents*

Note

This is the fourth case that I have thus far recorded from the files of the top-secret Omega organization, and for those among my readers who may not have seen the preceding volumes,* perhaps they deserve a few words of explanation.

My agreement with Prince Zarkon is simple and to the point: I will have full access to Omega's files, may select whichever cases I consider most bookworthy, and may conduct tape-recorded interviews with individuals involved, upon which to build my narrative.

But Zarkon believes, quite rightly, that Omega functions best when as little as possible is known about it. Therefore:

All of the names of people and places and institutions in this book are fictitious. There are, for example, no persons known to me who are named Prince Zarkon, Scorchy Muldoon, Nick Naldini, etc. Neither is there a Mayor Phineas T. Bulver or a city on the eastern seaboard called Knickerbocker City.

It has amused my readers (I hope) and myself (quite certainly) to borrow names of people and places from various sources, largely from the back issues of the old crime-fighter pulp magazines which I devoured in my early teens. The sources of some of these borrowings will be obvious to many of the more initiate of my readers, and I will not spoil your fun in figuring the others out by listing them all here. However:

Nita Van Sloan and the box of gold-tipped Dimitrios comes from one of the Spider novels, *Wings of the Black Death*.

* *The Nemesis of Evil, Invisible Death*, and *The Volcano Ogre* are their titles. All three were published in hardcover by Doubleday and reprinted in paperback by Popular Library.

Station WNX, the Knickerbocker City *Gazette,* the exclusive Cobalt Club, Miss Margo Lane and the investment broker, Rutledge Mann, come from several of the Shadow novels.

The vacant red brick house on the corner of Mountainair and Farmwell streets comes from the first of Lester Dent's remarkable Doc Savage novels, *The Man of Bronze.*

The scientists Hezekiah Spafford and Barton Swift come, respectively, from *Twelve Must Die,* a Doctor Death novel, and from the Tom Swift books.

The Belshazzar gun, the Empire Park Hotel, and the Golden Apple nightclub come from the first and only novel (*The Totem-Pole Murders*) in the only issue of an extremely rare and short-lived pulp called *The Angel.*

Dr. Alexei Zorka and the Amsterdam Fault come from a marvelous old Bela Lugosi movie called *The Phantom Creeps* (Universal Pictures, 1939).

I will leave it up to you to figure out the sources of the several people Prince Zarkon meets in the Cobalt Club in Chapter 4, and of the ladies who share a table with Phoenicia Mulligan in Chapter 1.

And you shouldn't have to be a trivia expert to realize the identity of the crippled newsboy who let Joey Weston borrow the bicycle he was taking care of for a friend.

I will save you a lot of time right now by admitting that I simply made up such names as Knickerbocker City, Mayor Bulver, Lucifer, Ching, and Fooey Mulligan. Not *every* name in the book was cleverly drawn from my vast, extensive reading.

Enjoy!

—*Lin Carter*

The Earth-Shaker

CHAPTER 1

When the Earth Shook

Miss Phoenicia Mulligan snuggled back in the cozy booth and relaxed with a weary sigh of relief. A busy morning of shopping in the department stores and boutiques of the fashionable Upper East Side of Knickerbocker City with her girl friends had resulted in the heap of gaily wrapped packages to her left.

"I," the pretty blond girl announced determinedly, "am going to have a dry martini."

"Yes, Miss," the hovering waiter acknowledged deferentially. "And you other ladies?"

Miss Margo Lane, the slim, dark-haired girl who sat across from "Fooey" Mulligan, decided on a daiquiri. Patricia Savage Hazzard, the striking bronze-haired young woman on Margo's left, opted for a margarita. Nita Van Sloan, the brunette socialite seated next to Fooey, chose an old-fashioned. As for Nellie Grey, she ordered a whiskey sour. The girls lit cigarettes, flexed weary feet, discussed their new hairdos animatedly.

The meeting between these old school chums was decidedly a rare event. That was primarily because Miss Phoenicia Mulligan customarily resided in California and seldom came east to the great metropolis beside the Atlantic. Learning that Fooey Mulligan was visiting Knickerbocker City this month, Mrs. Hazzard had contacted each member of the little group, inviting them to a morning "on the town" to welcome their chum.

The day had begun with an all-around beauty treatment at Mrs. Hazzard's famous establishment—Patricia, Incorporated—on Park

Avenue. Then had followed a tour of the most exclusive stores Knickerbocker City could offer to the discerning young woman of taste and considerable lucre—from Bonwit's and Bloomingdale's down to the little boutiques tucked away on the side streets. Their shopping concluded, the girls had decided on Schrafft's for a late lunch and cocktails.

Phoenicia was blissfully satisfied, and sipped her drink with the relish and gusto this adventure-loving young lady applied to nearly everything in life. Mrs. Hazzard, however, looked wistful.

"What's eating you, Pat?" demanded Fooey, tossing back her blond curls.

Margo Lane smiled slyly. "Probably, she's finally added up how much money she could have made on our beauty treatments if they hadn't been 'on the house,' " she grinned.

Pat looked rueful. "Nonsense—I don't even own it, anymore. Sold it when I married Rex. Still get my face done for free, of course—that was in the contract. *And* the right to treat my friends. No . . . I just wished I'd been able to get in touch with Muriel Havens and Doro Kelly, so they could've come along . . ."

"Probably a good thing you couldn't," quipped Nita Van Sloan wickedly. "Or we couldn't have all fitted into one booth. Come to think of it—we can't, as it is! Thank Heavens Nellie is so small, or we'd have to have the waiter pull up an extra chair."

Nellie Grey smiled calmly. The diminutive (but perfectly proportioned) young woman was well accustomed to jokes about her height. Then she sobered. "What about Carol Baldwin, Pat?"

"Couldn't get hold of her, either," the bronze girl sighed. "It's a shame; we could have had a real, full-fledged gathering of the clan—"

Phoenicia Mulligan reached over and squeezed her friend's hand. "Never you mind, Pat. It's been just swell, seeing all of you again, as it is. And maybe I'll stay here for a while and get to see Muriel and Doro and Carol another time . . . it all depends on that big, dumb, stubborn lug—"

Margo pretended to look scandalized. "Is that any way to refer to His Royal Highness?" she asked with mock incredulity.

The girls snickered at the mutely rebellious look that appeared on the attractive features of their visiting friend. It was common knowledge that, last month in the Luzon islands, in the Pacific, Fooey Mulligan had met—and fallen rather resoundingly for—the handsome, enigmatic adventurer who called himself Zarkon, who had formerly ruled the little Balkan state of Novenia, as its Prince, before abdicating.

It was also commonly known that Prince Zarkon, although completely masculine in his tastes, had a built-in immunity where girls were concerned—even strikingly beautiful girls of the likes of Fooey Mulligan.

"Never mind, Fooey, you'll wear him down in time," grinned Pat. "Look at me and Rex—*he* didn't think women should play any part in the lives of busy adventurers, either. But I got into his blood, in time."

"Oh, yeah?" Phoenicia bristled. "And what about *Doc?* Plenty of girls have been after his bronze hide, and he hasn't succumbed yet!"

"Touché," chuckled Pat, ruefully. Her famous cousin was of the same opinion as Captain Hazzard and Prince Zarkon, where women were concerned.

"Lamont and I—" began Margo.

"Richard and I—" began Nita in the same breath.

As her chums began animatedly discussing their gentleman friends, Phoenicia Mulligan found herself looking out through the front windows of the restaurant dreamily, thinking how long it had been since she had last visited Knickerbocker City. It occurred to her that if she intended to remain in the city for some time, which probably would be the case, she had better wire her bank on the Coast and arrange for the transferral of some of her funds to a banking establishment here.

This thought happened to occur to the blond girl because, directly across the street from the Schrafft's restaurant in which she and her friends were sitting, an imposing edifice of that nature rose ponderously, its classic marble façade discreetly bearing the name of the Jefferson National Bank and Trust Company.

And just as Phoenicia Mulligan was admiring the architecture of the bank, things began to happen.

A small van had pulled up before the restaurant only a moment or two before. It was painted a dark blue, and its sides were adorned with the legend JOE'S DIAPER SERVICE. It did not then occur to the blond girl to wonder what such a delivery truck would be doing parked on a street of distinctly *un*-residential nature.

She was more interested in the man who sat in the driver's seat.

He was a small, slight man of oriental race, probably Chinese. In itself, there was nothing curious about that, for the Chinese are an industrious people and are found in every imaginable business enterprise, not just in Chinese restaurants and Chinese laundries.

No—what caught Fooey Mulligan's eye was that she could have sworn she had seen the face somewhere—and in a context dramatically more sinister than merely as a truck driver. . . .

In the very next moment, her attention was torn from the half-shadowed face of the small Chinese and riveted again on the bank opposite the restaurant.

For the earth—shook. . . .

A deep, ominous rumble began far beneath the streets of Knickerbocker City. The sound grew rapidly louder, almost as if it were coming nearer.

With an ear-splitting shriek, the plate-glass window through which Fooey was staring cracked all the way across.

On the polished tabletop, the frosted glasses began to jiggle and dance, spilling their beverages.

A tremor passed through the floor, making their booth tremble.

Voices yelled in startled outcry, in surprise and in fear. From the rear of the restaurant there came a loud crash as a waiter dropped a heavily laden tray.

Fooey's attention was fixed, however, across the street.

A crack had widened in the asphalt wherewith the street was thickly coated. It began, apparently, in the very middle of the street, and zigzagged across to the pavement of the sidewalk on the opposite side of the street, where the Jefferson National Bank and Trust stood.

While the blond girl sat frozen, staring in blank amazement, the shock wave hit the front of the bank. And it . . . *crumbled.*

The elaborately carved marble façade simply came apart in flying shards and massive slabs. These crashed and clattered about the sagging, buckling sidewalk.

Then the two Corinthian columns which supported the now unadorned architrave began to lean and topple. One—the one to the right—fell all in one piece, as a tree falls when felled by loggers. It struck the roof of a long, sleek Supra limousine parked at the curb. The roof caved in; the windshield came apart in a spurting spray of pulverized glass.

The second column, however, came apart in four huge, round, drum-shaped segments which went rolling and bumping into the street.

In the next instant, the air shook from a long, shattering roar of sound as the building literally shook itself to pieces. The bright afternoon air became hazed with stone dust. Chips sprayed over the pavement and danced like water drops on a hot skillet.

The building caved *inward,* walls buckling. The shrieking hiss of escaping steam from a fractured water main ripped through the rumbling, crashing noise of the collapsing building.

Then the noise died away.

The ground no longer shook.

There arose a clamor of frightened voices, crying, screaming, imploring. People ran into the street from every direction. Cursing, perspiring freely, a blue-coated cop appeared, lustily bellowing at them to keep back.

The building (as one could see by this time, as the haze of dust settled to the ground) was almost completely demolished. Only one tottering portion of the rear wall and a stump of a side wall remained standing. All else was a crazy jumble of broken rock and shattered brick and crumpled plaster and twisted steel.

Fooey sat glued to the cracked window, still staring out upon the awful scene, motionless as if frozen.

Within the cab of the little blue delivery van, the Chinese driver, who had sat unmoving through the catastrophe, smiled a thin-lipped smile.

He clicked down the knob on his watch.

From her angle, Phoenicia Mulligan could see that it was one of those big turnip watches gamblers use at the racetrack to time the horses. What do they call them? *Oh, yes,* she thought dazedly, *a stopwatch.* . . .

Without so much as a sideways glance at the ruins of the bank, the driver turned on the ignition and released the clutch. Moving slowly through the shocked, murmuring mob of onlookers, the blue truck eased away from the curb and cruised off down the street, vanishing unobtrusively in the traffic.

As it went past her window, Phoenicia saw again the legend painted on its side: JOE'S DIAPER SERVICE.

Then it was gone.

The girls came out of Schrafft's and dug into the mob, volunteering their services to the perspiring officer. Some of them had taken classes in first aid, they informed the bluecoat.

"Begorra, missus, but it'll after bein' a blessin' if *any* o' them poor bahstids (beggin' yer pardon, ladies!) get outa that rubble alive, but stick aroun' . . ." he groaned, mopping his scarlet brow.

Within moments a police cruiser pulled up beside the crumpled limousine. Then another one, followed by an ambulance with lights flashing, siren shrilling. No longer needed, the girls retreated to the other side of the street. Pat paid the pale and shaking waiter; her chums gathered up their packages.

"Where's Fooey?" murmured Pat Hazzard, peering around.

"She hailed a cab," replied Margo, "and drove off. Somewhere on the West Side—I didn't hear the address."

"Hmm, that's odd," said Pat perplexedly. "Well, I'll see that her stuff gets back to the hotel—d'you remember where she's staying, Margo?"

"I do," diminutive Nellie Grey volunteered demurely. "At the Marlborough. If you like, Pat, I'm going that way and can easily drop Fooey's packages off on my way to Bleek Street."

"Fine, you do that," said Pat. Subdued by the shock of the catastrophe, the girls quietly bade each other good-bye and went off to their several destinations. Forgotten were their plans for drinks and dinner at the fashionable Club Galaxy, followed by a popular Broadway revue.

They would have been even more distressed, could they have known that the catastrophe which leveled the Jefferson National Bank and Trust was only the first link in a chain of calamities which would soon grip all of Knickerbocker City in a web of terror.

CHAPTER 2

At Omega Headquarters

As the Yellow Cab drove Phoenicia Mulligan across town by one of the streets which meandered through the green, heavily treed acreage of Olmsted Park, the blond girl leaned back against the vinyl upholstery, trying to catch her breath and steady her racing pulse, and striving also to sort out her jumbled thoughts.

Phoenicia knew very well that—somewhere—some*when*—she had seen the face of that truck driver before. She remembered his slight build, stooped shoulders, shaven pate, and even the pair of heavily lensed eyeglasses that had masked his slant-eyed gaze.

But—*where?*

Rapidly, the girl leafed through her mind. Many important businessmen and financiers back in her California home were of oriental extraction, but none of the men she had met socially was the same as the man whose face she had glimpsed in the cab of that blue van.

Fooey Mulligan grimly knew that it was very important that she remember where she had seen the Chinaman. For she had a hunch that all was not exactly kosher in the peculiar earthquake that had reduced the Jefferson bank to rubble.

For one thing—she had never *heard* of an earthquake hitting Knickerbocker City before, in all its long and distinguished history.

The cab maneuvered through the city streets, and the adventure-loving blond girl was alone with her puzzled thoughts.

On the Upper West Side of Knickerbocker City, a block of brownstone tenements rises near the river.

To the eye of the casual observer, there is nothing about any of the buildings in this block that makes it seem particularly different in any way from hundreds of other, similar neighborhoods in the metropolis. Battered ash cans stand between flights of front steps. Geraniums flower gaudily in window boxes. Chalked and numbered squares along the sidewalk denote the presence of playing children. Television antennas lean at crazy angles atop the connecting roofs. Shuttered windows, or windows with drawn blinds, or windows with lace curtains, stare out upon the row of buildings across the street. At the end of the block flow the blue waters of the Henry Hudson River, amid which a small, tree-grown island can be glimpsed; beyond rise the cliffy palisades of New Jersey.

Appearances, however, when carefully contrived, can indeed be deceiving. For the entire block is one gigantic, fortress-like building, faced with blind windows and false fronts. And behind that row of imitation façades lies hidden the headquarters of the world's smallest but most renowned crime-fighting organization: Omega.

Those ordinary-seeming windows are, in reality, heavy slabs of impenetrable plastic, optically ground to perfect transparency. Those seemingly flimsy brick walls conceal thick armor plate braced by powerful steel beams. Basement generators supply Omega headquarters with its own power, and huge fans and air-conditioning and -filtering equipment circulate pure air. An enemy, no matter what forces he might command, is hardly likely to penetrate those massive walls, or to infiltrate poisonous gas or deadly germs into the air supply, or to interfere with Omega's electricity.

Only two doors on the entire block may be opened at all. By one of them, a small, unobtrusive brass plate bears as legend but a single letter, in the Greek alphabet: *omega.*

The innocent-seeming, block-sized fortress is removed from city or state or even federal law, as are the embassies of foreign governments. Diplomatic immunity protects Omega headquarters from undesired search or entry, even by officers of the law armed with court documents.

Here, secret from all but a few highly-placed officials, reside the five men who compose the most powerful and effective private crime-fighting organization on earth today, and their Hindu servant, and their mysterious Master.

Herein, as well, are chemical laboratories, complicated electrical apparatus, criminological and scientific libraries, immense exhaustive files of the dossiers of tens of thousands of known criminals, banks of data-storing computers, and long-range sending and receiving instruments which can put the Omega men instantly in touch with every foreign capital.

Of the five Omega men, only one was "on duty" in the sumptuously appointed living room beyond the door marked by the brass plate. He was a small, trimly built man in turtleneck pullover and slacks, with fiery hair, snub nose, and eyes as blue as the lakes of Killarney. A former bantamweight boxer and all-around expert in fisticuffs and roughhouse, his name was Aloysius Murphy Muldoon —labeled "Scorchy" Muldoon by admiring sportswriters, from the sizzling velocity of his punches in the prize ring, which fairly "scorched" the air.

At the moment Phoenicia Mulligan's cab drew up in front of the door, Scorchy Muldoon, perspiring freely, was toweling his brick-red face after a workout in the basement gym adjoining his own suite of rooms. When the doorbell rang, the feisty little Irishman crossed the room to where a screen of ground glass and a control console were set in the wall beneath a priceless original oil by Van Gogh. He thumbed the switch, turned a dial, and the screen glowed with light and lifelike color, depicting the likeness-in-miniature of a striking blond girl who stood, tapping one foot impatiently, on the doorstep.

"Oh, fer th' *luvva—*" groaned the husky little bantamweight, with a comical grimace. Then he leaned forward and spoke into the microphone. "Cripes, Fooey, you back again?" he complained. "You know th' Chief sez ye're not t' be allowed inside. . . ."

To the girl on the doorstep, it was as if a disembodied voice had addressed her out of thin air. Glancing about and up, she located the microphone and televisor-camera discreetly concealed in the concrete decorations above the door. A look of wrathful determination stiffened her features. "You open this door, you pipsqueak Paddy," she demanded resolutely, "or you'll rue the day you didn't! I got news, I have—"

"Aw, lissen, I can't—the Chief sez—"

"Fooey on what the Chief 'sez,'" snarled the girl, unconsciously employing her favorite expletive, from which her nickname had long since been derived by friends. And in clear, ringing, and slightly breathless tones, the girl imparted an astounding statement composed of only twenty words:

"That earthquake that wrecked the Jefferson bank at noon was a phony—and I saw the crook that did it."

It was about an hour later at Omega headquarters. Seated fidgeting on one of the comfortable sofas drawn up before the heavily carved fireplace, Miss Phoenicia Mulligan was reassuring a truculent, suspicious, and slightly apprehensive Scorchy that he had done well to admit her to the inner sanctum despite the unequivocal orders from his mysterious Master. Scorchy remained unimpressed.

Opposite the girl, a lanky, Satanic individual stretched out his long legs and grinned nastily at his partner's discomfort. With his sallow features (which bore a startling resemblance to the actor John Carradine, famed for his screen portrayals of Count Dracula, the Transylvanian bloodsucker of sensational fiction), pointed goatee, waxed mustachios, and blue-black hair, he bore an aspect at once theatrical and sinister. A former stage magician, vaudeville escape artist and reformed cardsharp, this was Nick Naldini, another of the five Omega men.

Nick's main delight in life was the baiting of the feisty little prizefighter, whose Irish temper, always volatile, tended to ignite with almost spontaneous combustion under Naldini's needling.

"You'll catch it, Pint Size, when the Chief comes up," Naldini was gloating at the moment in his hoarse, whiskey-roughened voice. "Guess we can't leave you alone for a minute—first blond that walks by can wheedle her way in here without half trying—"

"Izzat so, you fugitive from the bottom line of a broken-down vaudeville bill," growled Muldoon, flushing, balling his leathery fists and starting to rise.

Phoenicia Mulligan looked apprehensive, as if expecting the two to be rolling on the floor, chewing off each other's ears or noses in a moment. The others gathered about the room, however, ignored the verbal bout with the nonchalance of long endurance. One of these was a huge, cheerful, dumb-looking man with outsized hands and feet and the dull-eyed, slab-sided face of an amiable half-wit. Again, appearances are highly deceiving, for this man is Theophilus "Doc" Jenkins, a mental marvel with a camera eye, a tape-recorder ear, and a computer mind. Nothing he has ever read or seen or heard cannot be instantly retrieved from his amazing memory.

Catching the look of apprehension on the blond girl's face, Doc Jenkins grinned oafishly. "It's okay, Miss Mulligan," he said cheerfully. "Them two is always at it. But they don't hardly mean nothin' by it at all."

"Right," a small, sour-faced man snapped waspishly, not deigning to look at the blond heiress. "Very seldom does any actual bloodshed accompany one of these bouts. Scorchy and Nick are all talk, no action."

The Italian magician and the little Irishman broke off their loud exchange of insults to glare at the man, who chuckled nastily, this being the effect he had desired to produce. As for Phoenicia, she smiled wanly at him, but he again avoided her eyes. This scrawny, peevish individual, a brilliant electronic genius named Mendel Lowell Parker—"Menlo" Parker to his friends—is famous among his fellow Omega men as a dedicated and devout misogynist. He affects to loathe and despise all women, but whether this is feigned or sincere remains open to doubt.

Seated at the end of the sofa was a tanned, fit, good-looking young man in aviator togs, named Francis "Ace" Harrigan. The annals of international aviation boast of few such crack test pilots and air aces as this smiling young fellow, whose guileless expression and athletic build and classically chiseled features have set many a girlish heart aflutter ere now.

Just then a tall, swarthy, turbaned man entered the room with a tray of beverages. Handing a cocktail to Miss Mulligan with a profound bow, the imperturbable Chandra Lal set the tray down on the coffee table situated between the sofas and was about to retire as noiselessly from the room as he had entered it, when he was hailed by Doc Jenkins.

"Hey, Chandra, is th' Chief coming, do you know?"

"The *sahib* will attend you presently," said the tall Rajput in flawless English. "He is still studying reports from the Richter Institute and striving to correlate their findings with those of his own instruments."

"See, I *tol'* ya th' Chief'd be innerestid is this case, Fooey," said Muldoon with a sniff in Naldini's direction.

"Then, you feel certain there *is* a case here?" inquired a quiet voice from behind them.

They turned quickly to greet the striking individual who had just entered the room unnoticed through a secret door behind the bookshelves, where a hidden elevator communicated with the underground laboratories.

And Phoenicia Mulligan paled, bit her lip, drew in a long, unsteady breath, eyes misting dreamily.

For it was Prince Zarkon—the Master of Omega.

CHAPTER 3

Ching

The Man of Mystery was an ordinary-looking man. At an inch or so over six feet, he was only slightly above the average height for a male of his race and apparent age. And although his body was superbly muscled and he possessed one of the most perfectly developed physiques in the world at that time, so evenly proportioned and symmetrical was his musculature that he did not appear exceptional to the glance of the casual beholder.

It was only at second or third glance that something about him arrested your attention. Perhaps it was the strange, tawny shade of his skin, or the classic if impassive and immobile regularity of his features, or the breadth of his nobly proportioned brow,* which

---

* I have met Prince Zarkon on several occasions, and personally interviewed him at length concerning those of his cases which I have been permitted to record. And I can testify to the fact that he seems like a perfectly ordinary man in the prime of life. Those fortunate enough to have seen him in action, however, describe the incredible feats of strength, endurance and skill of which he is capable. And despite his apparent youthfulness, he is somewhat more than one hundred years old, insofar as I have been able to discern from fragments of his past which he sketched out in conversation.

The full extent of his abilities—physical, mental, moral, spiritual and intellectual—has never been tapped.

The adventures to which I allude above have been recorded by me with the express permission and somewhat reluctant cooperation of the entire Omega organization.

They may be found in four books, *The Nemesis of Evil, Invisible Death, The Volcano Ogre,* and the present volume, *The Earth-Shaker.* All of these have been published by the firm of Doubleday and may be procured from that firm or from your public library, probably.

The "reluctance" of the Omega men to confide in me, alluded to above,

denoted a brain many times superior to the highest intellects of which the planet could boast. But, more than likely, it was his eyes which caught and held your fascinated gaze. They were striking: large, deeply-set, and wide apart under his towering brow, orbs of scintillant, intense, black magnetic fire. Those eyes could hypnotize a man at a glance.

The skull that housed that magnificently developed brain was totally bald, the baldness concealed under a hairpiece whose trim locks were gunmetal gray. And the splendid, tawny-skinned body was casually dressed in gunmetal gray corduroy slacks and jacket, with gray suede shoes and a dark wine-red turtleneck pullover.

Such a man was Zarkon, Lord of the Unknown, the Man from the Future!

He had been born in the year One Million A.D., the ultimate result of a program of genetically selective breeding conducted over thousands of generations. In that remote era, life on earth was nearly extinct. Pollution of air and water, wastage of natural resources, endless war and ecological damage had very nearly rendered the earth uninhabitable. Only in the artificial domed city of Polarion, in the northern polar regions, did there exist a haven of enlightened technological research. All else was sterile wilderness, whereover wandered dwindling hordes of savages.

The Great Brains of Polarion, supercomputers wherein the totality of human knowledge was preserved, had long since ascertained the root cause of the collapse of human civilization. Long before the age of Polarion, in the Twentieth Century, there had arisen, in the intervals between three ruinous global conflicts, criminal masterminds employing advanced scientific secrets to exploit the superstitious fears of the populace. When urban civilization collapsed, after the nuclear holocaust of the third global conflict, it was these sinister supermen of crime who had seized the reins of power during the chaos of plague and famine and lawlessness which followed the disintegration of all major governments. Considering this, the Great

_____

stems from their conviction that secrecy about their organization and its methods affords that organization the best protection from its enemies. But since these books are marketed as *fiction*, no one is likely to take them seriously anyway.

Brains resolved upon a daring venture to change the present by un-doing the past.

For a quarter of a million years they had selectively bred a race of supermen called Arkons to rule the dwindling remnants of man-kind. But this program had reached fruition too late, for the earth was nearly dead. Therefore the last of these experimental supermen, Arkon Z-1000, was sent back in time to the 1970s to prevent the rise to power of the scientific super-criminals.

Calling himself Zarkon, he materialized first in the small Balkan principate of Novenia, a tiny but strategically vital princedom which controlled the world's only known source of the rare heavy metal rhombium, needed for the generation of atomic power and the construction of nuclear warheads. The processes by which rhom-bium was refined were slow, imperfect and costly; but Zarkon swiftly introduced a process for the refinement of rhombium metal which was cheap, fast and simple.

Overnight, Novenia became wealthy and powerful; named a na-tional hero by the Novenian peoples, Zarkon became their prince, ruling them wisely and well for a few years, before abdicating his throne and setting up a perfect model democracy. Prince Zarkon then came to New York, where he set up Omega headquarters and began selecting the five lieutenants who were to aid him in his cru-sade against super-crime. A grateful Novenian Government granted him a hereditary title, ownership of the block of brownstones which form the present site of Omega headquarters, and title to the small island in the Hudson where Zarkon retains a private fleet of ships and submarines of advanced design—all of which are under the Novenian flag and are protected by diplomatic immunity from the intrusion of municipal police or federal agents, thus ensuring Zarkon perfect and complete privacy in which to prosecute his magnificent battle against super-crime.

To further these ends, each year the present democratic govern-ment of Novenia deposits in a numbered Swiss bank account ten million dollars in gold from which Prince Zarkon is free to draw whatever sums he may require.

Such is the astounding nature and origin of the Lord of the Unknown, the Nemesis of Evil, the Master of Fate; and it is known to only five men on earth.

In his quiet, controlled way, Zarkon greeted Phoenicia Mulligan and made her welcome to his headquarters. Nor did he utter any rebuke to Scorchy Muldoon for admitting her to these premises contrary to Zarkon's explicit instructions.

The Master of Fate had first made Phoenicia's acquaintance a few weeks previously, while investigating certain mysterious deaths on the remote island of Rangatoa, in the Pacific.† The young woman had in the course of those adventures become rather thoroughly smitten with the masculine charms of the Man of Destiny. As for Zarkon, he felt sincerely, as I have already stated, that his career was too filled with perils to be shared by a woman, and habitually steered clear of such romantic complications.

Fooey Mulligan, however, was, in her own, ladylike way, every bit as tough and determined as was Zarkon himself. For a month now she had besieged Omega headquarters without gaining entry. And at last she had found the key to unlock that fortress-like door!

"Now, Phoenicia, perhaps you will be good enough to tell me the news you believe to be valuable," suggested Zarkon reasonably, taking a seat across from the girl. Bursting with suppressed excitement, she described the scene of the bank's destruction, to which Zarkon listened attentively, without interrupting her somewhat confused account.

He appeared interested to hear her eyewitness account of the peculiar accident but did not seem particularly impressed. Other witnesses had been interviewed on the news programs of local television stations, and her account contained little that was new.

"The consensus," he commented gently, once the girl had finished, "seems to be that the destruction of the bank was caused by the explosion of an underground bomb or, perhaps, of a ruptured gas main. Authorities are still investigating; but the possibility of an earthquake having caused the accident is generally discounted.

† See the third of the adventures of Omega which I have recorded, published in book form as a novel under the title of *The Volcano Ogre* (1976).

Knickerbocker City is not in a known earthquake zone, and seismic convulsions of that caliber have never before been recorded in this state. . . ."

"I watched the whole thing," said Fooey, with flashing eyes. "And I know an earthquake when I see one!" Zarkon nodded soothingly, still apparently not impressed by her vehemence. Then it was that Fooey dropped her bombshell and described the slight, bespectacled Chinaman with the shaven pate who had timed the phenomenon with a stopwatch, then driven away.

At this, Zarkon's eyes narrowed ever so slightly: The behavior of the Chinese driver *was* a bit peculiar.

"The gal thinks she recognized this gink, Chief," spoke up Doc Jenkins excitedly.

"Yeah, while we wuz after waitin' fer ya, I took her t' the file room and we went through book after book a' photographs," added Scorchy Muldoon.

"And did Phoenicia identify the person she observed in the blue panel truck?" asked Zarkon.

Scorchy nodded triumphantly. "She did that," the bantamweight Hibernian burbled.

"Not only that, Chief," thrust Naldini, deftly inserting himself into the exchange. "Not only that, but I checked the City Directory and there is no such firm as Joe's Diaper Service listed anywhere in the five boroughs. . . ."

"She picked out *Ching*, Chief," snapped skinny little Menlo Parker, his eyes sparkling with excitement.

Zarkon said nothing, but his face became as impassive as a mask.

Ching was a former henchman of the brilliant but deranged scientist Lucifer.

Zarkon and the Omega men had crossed swords with Lucifer on a previous occasion or two, and knew him for a clever, resourceful and dangerous opponent. Fortunately, the mad scientist had met his doom at the terminus of their last engagement. Ching, however, was known to be still alive. . . .

At Zarkon's request, Nick put through a radiophone call to the federal penitentiary in California where the subtle Oriental was presumably incarcerated. He returned from the call with a glum expression on his usually sardonic features.

Ching had escaped during a fire in the prison at which inmates had joined the guards as volunteer fire fighters. The conflagration was presumed to have been the work of an arsonist.

No trace of the fugitive had yet been found.

Which made it quite possible that the man Phoenicia Mulligan had seen near the Jefferson National Bank just before its destruction had, after all, been Ching.

Zarkon looked grim.

If Ching had escaped, might not it be that his master, far cleverer than he, had also escaped the certain death to which had Zarkon believed him doomed?

And if Lucifer lived, there was plenty of good reason for the Prince to look grim.

For Lucifer, master of evil science, was one of the most dangerous men on the planet.

CHAPTER 4

File Z-9

Leaving Omega headquarters in one of his private cars, Prince Zarkon crossed town and parked before a handsome old building on one of the side streets off Fifth Avenue. The marble façade, the dignified, silver-haired doorman, and a discreetly lettered bronze plaque all announced that this was the Cobalt Club, one of the most fashionable and exclusive social clubs in Knickerbocker City. Its members were drawn from the ranks of the oldest, wealthiest, most socially prominent families, and from men of unusual importance or distinction. Zarkon had been elected to membership the first year he lived in the city. He found its members generally well-informed sources of reliable information, due to their intimate connections with the sources of wealth, industry and political power.

Entering the spacious lounge, he discovered a number of men chatting together in comfortable chairs over afternoon cocktails. He nodded in reply to their greetings, and paused by two of them who were seated together. Both gentlemen were immaculately attired and well past their youth. One sported a jaunty, trim mustache, while the other wore a monocle.

"Good afternoon, Philo, Nick," he greeted these acquaintances. "I was hoping Dr. Littlejohn would be in here. Have either of you happened to see him?"

Mr. Charles and Mr. Vance suavely denied having seen the distinguished geologist. "One of the crew of that Savage fella, isn't he?" drawled Vance interrogatively. "Seen him around the clubs."

Zarkon assured the aristocratic Mr. Vance that William Harper

Littlejohn did indeed have that affiliation. The dapper, debonair Mr. Charles—Park Avenue visible in him from the part in his hair to the spats on his highly polished footwear—then inquired as to whether Zarkon had looked for him in the library. Zarkon had not, and went at once to see if the visitor he expected was there.

He was indeed, and a peculiar-looking gentleman he was, stooped over a weighty scientific tome, his gray-brushed hair falling across his bulging brow, his arms and legs like sticks. Zarkon greeted him quietly and they shook hands.

"Wasn't that Weizmann's treatise on parapsychology you were glancing at just now?" inquired Zarkon. The lanky scarecrow with the thin and graying locks snorted derisively.

"Unequivocally," he sneered. "And a superfarrago of cabalistically obreptitious quasi-data, obfuscated by a perennial and intrinsic occultation of the cerebrum—"

Zarkon repressed a slight smile. "I take it you consider the work a needlessly complicated jumble of half-facts, confusingly interpreted by a scholar with a lame brain?" he inquired.

"Johnny" Littlejohn looked nonplussed. It was seldom that he encountered anyone able to sight-read (as it were) the long words he usually sprinkled through his conversation. Indeed, he looked a trifle sheepish.

"I'll be superamalgamated," he murmured faintly. And thereafter, with an almost visible effort, the other man kept his remarks as monosyllabic as possible.

"I took a chance that you might be in town," Zarkon began, once they were comfortably settled in easy chairs in a dim corner of the library where they were unlikely to be disturbed. "And invited you here because I wish to confirm a few impressions of my own regarding the local history of seismic activity. Am I correct in assuming that Knickerbocker City has never experienced an earthquake of major proportions?"

Johnny opened his mouth to say something like "Unequivocally," looked ashamed, and said instead, "That's right."

"Then, the force which destroyed the Jefferson National this noontime was, must have been, other than seismic and natural?"

"I suppose so . . . what was the Richter reading, do you know?"

Zarkon told him, and the lanky scientist pursed his thin lips judiciously but refrained from comment.

Zarkon pressed him still further for his considered opinion on the possibility of an earthquake having been the cause of the bank's collapse. Johnny looked stubborn.

"The city rests on solid rock," he said. "Solid bedrock of granite. And the structure of the tectonic plates along the North Atlantic coastal regions simply do not conform to the configuration you find in earthquake-prone places like California or Japan."

"Is it, then, your considered professional opinion that no natural earthquake could possibly occur in Knickerbocker City or environs?" Zarkon pressed him.

Johnny Littlejohn fidgeted, looked unhappy. "Wellll . . ." he drawled.

Zarkon waited patiently. The lanky scarecrow rubbed one hand through his tumbled gray hair and squinted at Zarkon through the monocle he wore, which was affixed to his lapel by a black silk ribbon. Then he dug out a pocket notebook, scribbled something in it, tore out the page, folded it in half, and thrust it into Zarkon's hand.

Then he jumped up and virtually bolted from the room, leaving a trail of stammered apologies behind him.

Zarkon looked after the skinny geologist thoughtfully.

Just at that moment, an urbane, rotund man with a healthy tan and silvery hair entered the room and crossed to where Zarkon sat.

"Prince Zarkon?" he inquired pleasantly. "My name is Rutledge Mann. I believe you left an urgent call at my office, requesting me to attend you here."

"That's right, Mr. Mann, and thank you for coming on such short notice," said the Prince, shaking hands.

"Are we acquainted, sir?" continued Mann. "I generally know most of my clients personally—an investment consultant really must, you know—but there are always a few who dwell in more distant parts . . . ?"

"I have not had that pleasure, no," the Prince stated. "But we have a mutual friend in Mr. Cranston, of Merwyn, New Jersey, one of my fellow members here at the Cobalt Club—"

"Ah, Lamont: to be sure!" said Rutledge Mann with a genial nod. "Very well, then; how may I be of service to Your Highness?"

"The Jefferson National Bank," said Zarkon quietly. "What do you know of its management?" The stockbroker blinked.

"In the financial world, no one is considered more highly than Mr. Carleton Earnshaw, the director," he said expansively. "A gentleman of good family, background and breeding, and of the highest integrity, I can assure you."

Zarkon nodded, making no comment. "One hears, these days, of occasional bank failures—" he began.

But Rutledge Mann cut him off with a gesture. "Out of the question, my dear sir, in the case of the Jefferson," he said decisively. "Assets of over one hundred million, and never the slightest shakiness on the Market. Know their holdings well, for another of my clients, Mr. Bruce Wayne, of—ah? you know him?—well, anyway. You may put your mind at rest, if you are troubled by any thoughts that, just possibly, the explosion was—ah—*contrived*."

The broker continued to hold forth on the soundness of the Jefferson National and on the scrupulous integrity of its director, Mr. Carleton Earnshaw, for some moments, citing facts and figures and rattling off statistics with a sure and steady knowledge.

They parted, and Zarkon returned to the lounge. Spotting another acquaintance, in a window seat, studying with an expression of quiet and superior amusement the front pages of a leading daily of the financial world, he strolled over and greeted the other.

"It's good to see you again, Gorman," he said, shaking the hand held out to him. "I was just talking with Rutledge Mann about the Jefferson Bank and its director, and he assured me that everything was on the up-and-up with both."

"Cash" Gorman, the notorious Wizard of Wall Street, grinned cynically. "A stodgy old conservative, Mann is," he confided to Zarkon. "And generally we are on the opposite sides of the street on such questions—he regards me as an entrepreneur, little more than an adventurer!—but, in this case, Prince, I have to agree with the old boy."

"You mean—?"

"The Jefferson had assets which are not to be sneezed at," said Gorman with a shrewd wink. "Solid as the proverbial Rock of G. And I have never heard the slightest whisper of a rumor about Carleton Earnshaw. He's straight as straight can be."

Zarkon thought for a moment, then tried a shot in the dark. "With all that integrity and all those moral scruples," he inquired, "what would a man like Earnshaw do if someone attempted blackmail—threatened to destroy the bank, or something?"

"Tell him to go to the Devil," declared Cash Gorman without a moment's hesitation.

"Thank you very much. Nice to see you again," said Zarkon, taking his leave.

On his way out of the lounge he waved good-bye to Nick Charles and Philo Vance. Pausing a moment in the lobby, the Prince dug out of his pocket the folded note William Harper Littlejohn had thrust into his hand, and for the first time opened and read it.

It was remarkably brief, and very cryptic.

ASK THE MAYOR TO SHOW YOU FILE Z-9, the note read.

Leaving the Club, Zarkon entered his car and sat there thinking for a moment.

Nick Naldini, on this occasion serving as Zarkon's driver, glanced at him in the rearview mirror.

"Where to, Chief?" he inquired. "Back to headquarters?"

"No," said Zarkon firmly. "Drive me down to City Hall, Nick, if you will."

"City Hall?" repeated the magician in mystified tones.

"City Hall," said Zarkon firmly.

"What *for?*" burst out the other.

"I'm not really sure," confessed Zarkon with a slight smile. "We will learn that, perhaps, when we get there. . . ."

All the way downtown, Naldini shook his head and grumbled audibly about "keeping secrets from people."

Zarkon said nothing.

CHAPTER 5

Scorchy Is Abducted

While Nick Naldini drove his Chief south to City Hall, Zarkon used the radiophone in his car to call Omega headquarters. It was his notion to open a second line of inquiry, and he directed Scorchy Muldoon to visit the bank director, Carleton Earnshaw.

Scorchy was delighted at the prospect of a little action. The peppery Hibernian was easily bored between cases, and begrudged Nick's role as the Chief's driver. The fact that the long-legged stage magician was often selected for this role rankled the soul of the little boxer. He was frequently heard to complain that Prince Zarkon should—at least occasionally—let *him* serve as his driver; and loudly demanded of heaven to know why this never happened.

"Prob'ly 'cause the Chief wants to get there in one piece," snorted Menlo Parker *sotto voce*. Scorchy shot a fierce glare in the little scientist's direction. The remark had sounded to him suspiciously like a dirty crack.

"You ain't castin' aspersions on me drivin' ability, are ye?" he demanded of the other.

"Who—*me?*" Parker inquired rhetorically, assuming an expression of virtually cherubic innocence, and casting his gaze heavenward as if in protest of this misreading of his meaning.

The fact of the matter was, of course, that Scorchy was just about the worst driver any of them had ever encountered. If there was a pedestrian anywhere within half a mile of Scorchy when he was behind the wheel, his vehicle would find a way to come so close to the unfortunate individual as to scare him out of a year's growth, even if the car had to climb the sidewalk and go through a hedge or two in order to accomplish this.

Scorchy's attitude toward cars was one of belligerent stubbornness, verging on apoplexy. In his heart of hearts the little Irishman was convinced that automobiles had a mind of their own and were out to make him look bad. For this reason, when you drove with Muldoon it was wise to have your insurance premiums paid well in advance.

"I'll go with you," said Phoenicia Mulligan firmly, ignoring the frantic signals of Doc Jenkins and Menlo Parker. The blond girl had found one or another excuse to hang around headquarters ever since Zarkon and Nick had driven off. Obviously, once her foot was firmly lodged in the door, the heiress figured to keep it there as long as possible. Chandra Lal, learning that she had missed her luncheon, had whipped up a delicious snack in record time. Exclaiming over Chandra's shrimp salad, cucumber soup and stuffed tomatoes, Phoenicia flattered the Hindu by declaring that Oscar of the Waldorf could do no better. Since finishing her lunch, though, the girl had gotten the itch to partake in this adventure, and when Zarkon instructed Scorchy to interview Carleton Earnshaw, Phoenicia jumped upon this opportunity to join in the fun with both feet, as it were. She knew she could twist the fiery-thatched little fighter around her pinky, for Muldoon had an eye for the girls.

They left together, descending to the basement garage by a high-speed elevator. Strutting importantly, Scorchy selected Zarkon's sleek, super-powered limousine for the trip. A radio signal from the dashboard opened the false front which concealed the garage exit, and Scorchy zoomed out, narrowly missing a lamppost, turned into the street with an unearthly screech of tortured gears, blithely turned the wrong way into a one-way street, ran through two red lights in a row, and nearly ran down a delivery boy on a bicycle.

"You ain't sayin' much," growled Scorchy suspiciously.

"I'm saving my breath for prayers," said Phoenicia, in a small, tight voice. Her eyes were squeezed shut, her features were white

under her California tan, and she was mentally reviewing the several bequests in her will.

Earnshaw lived to the north of Knickerbocker City, in the more
fashionable parts of the borough of Pelham. It had already been ascertained that, contrary to his regular habits, the bank director had
been absent from his office all that day and was presumably to be
found at his residence.

Somehow or other, Scorchy managed to get through the maze of
streets and across the river into Pelham without slaughtering or
maiming any pedestrians—although there were more than a few
who encountered the crazily careening limousine that afternoon
whose nerves would never quite be the same again—and pulled into
the driveway of the Earnshaw home, splattering the lawn and garden with a machine-gun-like hail of ricocheting gravel. Scorchy
hopped out cheerfully, wondering why smoke and steam were pouring from beneath the limousine's hood. On the opposite side,
Phoenicia crawled shakily out and stood there uncertainly, with the
aspect of a doomed mariner who had never really expected to see
dry land again and was dazed by his miraculous survival.

Mr. Earnshaw was not at home, the frosty butler informed them
with thin-lipped civility, but a rapid glimpse at some of the creden-
tials in Scorchy's wallet worked a magical transformation. Like all of
the Omega men, Scorchy carried an assortment of "To whom it may
concern" letters, in a secret compartment of his wallet, whose signa-
tures were guaranteed to wring cooperation from even the dourest
citizen. Various of these notes bore such letterheads as Gracie Man-
sion, the Governor's office, the White House and the office of the
Secretary-General of the United Nations. Others bore even more
impressive headings, such as Buckingham Palace.

The suddenly amenable butler ushered Scorchy and the girl into
a dim study, where Earnshaw sat staring numbly into a television
set. The news commentator was giving a reprise on the calamity
which had rocked the banking world. Earnshaw raised pale, twitch-
ing features to his unexpected guests, and shook hands with
Scorchy.

The little Irishman noticed that the banker's hands were damp with perspiration and that they trembled uncontrollably. Guessing that Carleton Earnshaw was badly shaken by the events of the day, Scorchy belligerently pressed the psychological advantage and fired off a rapid series of questions.

The banker wearily rubbed his eyes with sensitive fingers and nodded gloomily in response to Scorchy's questions.

"You are perfectly correct, Mr. Muldoon," he said in a listless whisper. "There was indeed a blackmail attempt, or—perhaps more accurately, an attempt at extortion."

Scorchy rubbed his hands together briskly. "Oboyoboyoboy!" he chortled gleefully. "Got the note about, have yez?"

Earnshaw took it from a wall safe and handed it to Zarkon's lieutenant.

"Typed," muttered Muldoon thoughtfully. "Jeepers! A million clams, eh? No piker, this yegg—"

"Signs himself 'the Earth-Shaker,'" mused Phoenicia Mulligan interestedly, peering over Scorchy's shoulder. "Threatens to destroy the Jefferson National Bank by one o'clock this afternoon if you don't meet his demands. I gather you said 'no' to this request, eh?"

The banker looked down his nose at the blond girl severely. "I made no reply whatsoever," he stated evenly. "It is not in my character to yield to criminous extortion, or to—ah—knuckle under to such threats. . . ."

"Bank's prob'ly insured against sich Acts a' God as earthquakes, right?" inquired Scorchy shrewdly.

Looking wan, the banker nodded wearily. "The monetary loss is of no importance," he admitted. "What cannot, however, be repaired is the tragic loss of life . . . the responsibility for those deaths rests squarely upon my own shoulders. And I shall never be able to forgive myself—"

"For not paying the money?" asked Phoenicia Mulligan.

The banker shook his head woefully. "For not closing the bank today," he sighed heavily. "But I never actually dreamed there was any substance to these wild threats. I thought them the work of a madman."

After a few more questions, Scorchy and Phoenicia left and began to drive back to Knickerbocker City.

They did not notice the dark, ordinary-looking sedan following them until, on a deserted stretch of country road, it drew up alongside and two men leaned out with revolvers in their fists and fired point-blank at Scorchy.

When Scorchy Muldoon and Phoenicia Mulligan did not return to Omega headquarters, Ace and Doc and Menlo thought little of it.

"Probably got hauled into traffic court," chuckled Doc Jenkins after a glance at his watch showed the pair more than half an hour late. "Scorchy musta tried fer a shortcut and drove through a coupla storefronts."

"Either that or ran down a motorcycle cop," said Menlo Parker nastily. "No word from th' Chief, either; right?"

"He went to the Cobalt Club to talk to Dr. Littlejohn and that banker friend of Cranston's, Rutledge Mann," volunteered Ace Harrigan cheerfully. "Be back any time now, most likely."

Just then, the shortwave crackled from wall speakers, and a breathless feminine voice began speaking in mid-remark.

"*. . . how you work this dang thing, anyway! Ace? Doc? Menlo? Have I got it tuned in right?*"

"That's Miss Mulligan's voice," gasped Menlo Parker, turning pale as milk. "There musta been trouble of some kind!" The skinny little scientist—who swore he hated women worse than poison but was always among the first to spring to their defense when danger threatened—came out of his easy chair as if galvanized. He spun the dials on the communications console desperately, as Fooey's voice faded in a crackle of static.

"Miss Mulligan?" the waspish little scientist called urgently. "Menlo Parker here. What's happened? *Where's Scorchy?*"

"*. . . dang thing . . . Menlo? . . . Scorchy was carried off by a carful of thugs. Followed us from Carleton Earnshaw's house—dark sedan—fired a couple of shots, but they bounced off those trick windshields you boys have. Then they rammed us and we ended up*" *in a ditch. I got knocked in the head, and when I got back to my senses, they were driving off with Scorchy."*

Menlo slapped his imposing brow with the palm of one hand, a gesture characteristic with the elderly scientist when in moments of extreme worry or stress. Rapidly instructing the blond girl to take a cab back to Omega headquarters, Menlo snapped off the radio and turned to inform Ace Harrigan of these events.

"Who'd want to put the snatch on Scorchy?" murmured the aviator wonderingly. "Guess there must be some gang mixed up in this caper, after all. . . . Well, what do we do about it, Menlo?"

"We go huntin'," snapped the other. "Ace, get a car!"

CHAPTER 6

The Empty House

Zarkon was returning to Omega headquarters when Menlo Parker called him on the two-way car radio to inform him of Scorchy's abduction. The Omega Man frowned grimly, once he had abstracted from Parker all relevant information.

"Trace them to their hiding-place, Menlo," he instructed, "but do not attempt a rescue on your own. I will follow shortly. Who has remained behind to hold down the fort?"

"*Doc is still there, and Chandra Lal, of course,*" said the radio voice. "*Doc wanted to come along like crazy, but I thought we might need a backup force in case things got hot.*"

"Quite right, Menlo. Keep in touch," said Zarkon, turning off the set.

Nick Naldini swore feelingly at the news, and the knuckles of his hands, clenching the steering wheel of the car, were bone-white from the tension. Zarkon said nothing: He knew the warm and very deep friendship between the unlikely pair, despite their continuous verbal scrapping, and sympathized.

Arriving at Omega headquarters, the Prince wasted no time informing Doc Jenkins of the discovery he had made at City Hall.

The big, dull-eyed man looked puzzled, hearing what Zarkon had to tell him concerning the contents of the mysterious Z-9 file. He rubbed a huge hand slowly across the top of his head, as if thereby to somehow stimulate the mental processes.

"Well, Chief, sure . . . I heard of this guy, Dr. Alexei Zorka . . .

he was around back in the thirties, geologist of some note, wacky inventor-type . . . but I never heard of anything about the—"

"Seemingly, it was hushed up at the time," explained Zarkon. "Very little concerning the subject ever got out; even the newspapers were muzzled. I presume to avoid a panic among real estate speculators if the truth became known."

"Yeah, it would sure do *that*," commented the other dazedly.

Just then, Fooey Mulligan pulled up before the building in a cab and came in seething. Zarkon asked her for further information about Scorchy's abductors.

"Just ordinary-looking mugs," the blond girl said peevishly. "And I barely got a glimpse of their car, dark sedan, nothing special about it—what gets my goat is, I bumped my head on the dashboard when they rammed us, and missed the whole fight!"

Nick Naldini grinned sourly: When Scorchy Muldoon got into a free-for-all, the spectacle was not one to be missed. He would like to have observed it himself.

The girl looked around at them. "Well, why are you birds just sitting there?" she demanded. "Why aren't you out trying to rescue Scorchy?"

"Everything that can be done is already being done," the Man of Mystery said quietly. "Ace and Menlo are on the trail."

"On the trail of *what?*" the girl asked in an exasperated tone of voice. "How do they know what car Scorchy's in, or where it's going?"

In brief, soothing words, Nick Naldini informed the young woman that Scorchy, like all of the Omega men, carried a 'tracer' secreted on his person. The small, unobtrusive device emitted a constant radio signal which could be followed and its location pinpointed by means of the directional apparatus Ace Harrigan and Menlo Parker had taken with them in the car.

Phoenicia Mulligan flopped disgustedly down on a sofa and lit a cigarette. "Okay, we just sit around on our duffs and wait, I guess!" she murmured.

Doc Jenkins came shuffling in with a file folder in one large hand. He showed it to Zarkon.

"Here's the dope on this guy Zorka," said the big man. "He was quite an inventor in his time, it seems. *Time* did a profile on him, claimed he was up there with such big-league brains as Hezekiah Spafford or Barton Swift . . . came to an obscure end, something about an airplane accident."

Zarkon skimmed quickly through the material, nodding thoughtfully. "It appears that he entertained a number of dubious theories, which made him colorful fodder for reporters of the more sensational dailies, but of questionable reputation among his fellow scientists," he mused.

"What are you boys talking about?" inquired Miss Mulligan suspiciously. Zarkon explained to her about the note from Littlejohn and the enigmatic file kept under lock and key in the wall safe in the office of the Mayor of Knickerbocker City.

"Well, what's the file about? What does it have to say?" she demanded; Fooey Mulligan hated being left out of things, and she smelled an adventure in this case which she was determined to participate in.

Zarkon, however, declined to answer her question, being equally determined to keep her out of the caper.

Just then, the radio cleared its throat, and Menlo Parker made his report.

". . . *Chief?*"

"I am right here, Menlo. Any news?"

"Yep. We followed Scorchy's 'tracer' to a vacant red brick house on the corner of Mountainair and Farmwell streets. That's uptown, in a seedy residential area. You take Fifth Avenue north—"

"I know the neighborhood," said Zarkon. "How do you know the house is vacant?"

"Well, coupla windows are busted out on the second floor, and there's a 'For Rent' sign stuck in the front yard," Menlo answered.

"Keep the house under observation," the Master of Men told him, "but don't try anything on your own. We'll be there shortly."

Fooey jumped up, grabbing her purse. "Let's go!" she said excitedly.

Zarkon shook his head firmly. "We are going, but I want you to stay right here," he said in a level tone of voice that did not permit argument.

"And miss all the fun?" the blond girl wailed.

"We need someone here to keep an eye on things," Doc Jenkins pointed out diplomatically. "S'pose one of us calls for help on the radio?"

"Chandra Lal can—"

"Chandra Lal has his own duties," said Zarkon.

And that was that. As she watched them drive away, Fooey wrinkled up her attractive features into a ferocious scowl.

"Fooey!" said Fooey to herself.

During the drive uptown, Zarkon used the radio-telephone in the car to call Rutledge Mann at his offices in the Badger Building. He asked the broker to inquire among his friends in the banking community to see if any of them had received extortion notes similar to the one Carleton Earnshaw had shown Scorchy Muldoon and Phoenicia Mulligan.

The broker promised to circulate inquiries and said that he would call back as soon as he had managed to learn anything of interest. Prince Zarkon gave him the call number of the car radiophone and thanked him.

The big car nosed into a disreputable neighborhood of run-down buildings and ramshackle homes. The neighborhood seemed slumping into decay and largely abandoned, and was obviously slated for urban renewal. They pulled up around the corner from the red brick house and parked out of sight.

Leaving the car, the Omega men joined Menlo Parker and Ace Harrigan, who had parked their own vehicle behind a boarded-up grocery store. Zarkon instructed them in his plan while they circled the block, nearing the brick house.

"If we attempt to rush the house, Scorchy may be harmed," he said somberly. "Therefore, we shall employ other means."

Stationing his men where they could not be seen but could keep an eye on the front and back doors, Zarkon went down an alley and climbed a rust-eaten fire escape to the roof of the adjoining building.

He then made his way across the cracked tarry rooftop to the side nearest to the house and peered over the ledge. The peaked roof of the red brick house was three stories lower than the roof of the building he had climbed, but the Nemesis of Evil had no intention of trying to jump to the next building. Instead, he removed from his jacket a peculiar apparatus which rather resembled the air gun used by spearfishers, except that a bulky reel of metal cord was attached to the end of the spear.

This he carefully aimed and pressed the trigger. With a slight cough of compressed air, the projectile was launched. Like a pronged metal arrow, it whizzed across the space to attach itself to the chimney of the house.

Zarkon unfastened the end of the line and made it secure to one of the chimneys of the roof upon which he stood. Then, testing the tightly stretched cord to make certain it would bear his weight, he donned a pair of heavy protective gloves and swung over the ledge.

With the agility of an acrobat, the Man from Tomorrow swung hand over hand, feet dangling in empty air, and soon gained the roof of the brick house.

Menlo had been right about the broken windows. Obviously, mischievous neighborhood boys had broken them with thrown stones, as is the way with boys universally. Zarkon entered the house by means of one such and found himself in an empty room. Plaster was flaking from the ceiling, and strips of faded wallpaper were peeling from the walls. A few pieces of cheap, broken furniture stood in the corner, and the floor was covered with soiled linoleum.

Zarkon went to the door and peered out into the hall, his steps making no sound, due to the rubber-soled shoes he was wearing. The hall was also empty, and the house seemed to breathe a melancholy air of long abandonment. From small pockets in the lining of his jacket, Zarkon produced a device which he placed in his ears. Adjusting the dial, he employed the instrument like a sensitive stethoscope. Nowhere on the top floor did he detect the presence of men.

Even men who are trying to keep silent make small, unconscious sounds, he well knew. They clear their throat, they shuffle their feet, boards creak underfoot as they change position—and the electronic device which enhanced his hearing a thousandfold was fully capable of detecting such sounds.

As noiselessly as possible, Zarkon descended the stair to the second floor. Again he could not detect any sounds denoting a living presence.

Descending to the first floor, he was looking about carefully when a voice, startlingly loud due to the super-stethoscope in his ears, boomed suddenly from behind him.

"Well, Chief, I wuz wonderin' how long before one o' you guys'd show up," said Scorchy Muldoon.

CHAPTER 7

The Second Threat

Looking disgusted with himself, the feisty redhead was tied with a length of clothesline to a kitchen chair. Zarkon looked him over but could discern no signs denoting a struggle—which was unlikely, knowing Scorchy's penchant for fisticuffs.

"Never got a chance to lay a finger on th' lugs, Chief," he groaned aggrievedly. "Soon as I hopped outa th' car, one of 'em shot me in me arm wid a dart!"

"Some sort of anaesthetic, I suppose?" asked the Prince as he deftly untied the ropes.

Scorchy stood up, briskly massaging his arms and legs to aid the return of his circulation.

"Nope, sodium pentothal, I figger," he groused. "Sure made me spill my guts . . . 'fraid I answered every dadblame question they asked—"

"What did the men want to know?"

Scorchy shrugged. "How much Earnshaw tol' me, and what you were doin' about it. Since I didn't know that, I couldn't tell 'em anything—just about Earnshaw."

"How long ago did they leave?" asked Zarkon.

"Dunno," answered the Irishman. "I wuz so woozy from the truth-serum, I couldn't tell."

While Scorchy rubbed his arms and legs, Zarkon quickly but effectively searched the ground floor and basement of the abandoned house, finding little. There were recently smoked cigarette butts on the linoleum floor of the kitchen, where they had interrogated

Scorchy, but he found nothing else which the men had left behind them.

"Find somethin'?" inquired Muldoon.

Zarkon indicated the crushed cigarettes. "Mostly ordinary brands, Camels and Lucky Strike," he said. "The only surprise was this one—" He held it out for Scorchy to examine.

"A gold-tipped Dimitrio, huh?" said the ex-prizefighter puzzledly. "They're pretty expensive. Imported, too! Funny, for a ordinary mug to smoke imported Dimitrios. . . ."

"Had you ever seen any of the men before?" inquired Zarkon. Scorchy shook his head. "Just a buncha regular joes t' me," he added. "But the dope on the dart knocked me for a loop so darned fast, I didn't get a good look at all of 'em."

"How many were in the car?"

"Guess there was four or five," said Scorchy.

They left the house by the front door, which was unlocked, and were joined by their excited friends. Naldini pretended to look disgruntled that Scorchy had not been roughed up by his abductors.

"Thought at least they'd enjoy the opportunity of belting you a few times," he said yearningly. "Matter of fact, I'd have been happy to lend a hand—"

"Oh, yeah?" sneered Muldoon. "You ain't got a good belt in ya, ya skinny stage ham!"

Zarkon showed the cigarette he had found to Menlo, who examined it puzzledly.

"Odd choice of smoke for a bunch of mugs," commented the waspish scientist. "I got the feeling they don't exactly sell Dimitrios at every corner newsstand . . . maybe we could trace the cigarettes somehow, if only one or two shops sell 'em?"

"It's worth a try, I suppose," said Zarkon briefly.

They got in their cars and drove back toward headquarters. Zarkon checked the panel of his machine and found that a message had come in, on the radiophone, which the recorder had taken. He played the message back and was informed by the genial voice of the investment broker, Rutledge Mann, that at least one of his colleagues in the banking community was believed to have received a threatening message of some sort, possibly identical to the one given to Carleton Earnshaw.

". . . *Mr. Wentworth Blair, the managing director of the State Fidelity Trust Company,*" said the voice in the recording.

"That's on Herkimer Street, as I recall," murmured Ace Harrigan. "Want me to drive there now?"

Zarkon shook his head. "Banks close at three in the afternoon, and it's well past that by now," he said. "Let's return to headquarters."

Back at Omega headquarters, Zarkon's five lieutenants got to work. While Nick Naldini consulted tobacco importers on the phone, hoping to find who distributed gold-tipped Dimitrios in the city, Menlo tried to get in touch with Wentworth Blair. The wealthy banker was not listed in any of the city's telephone directories, which implied that, like many another important or influential man, he probably had an unlisted number.

Zarkon had a copy of the little-known "X-Directory," a full list of all publicly "unlisted" numbers—a volume also owned by the Mayor, the Police Commissioner, and the local office of the Federal Bureau of Investigation—so it was not difficult to find Wentworth Blair's number.

"He has a suite at the Marlborough, on South Olmsted Park," Menlo informed the Prince. "I been ringin', but he seems to be out—"

He broke off as Scorchy Muldoon came into the room, his face beaming excitedly. "He sure *is* out, Menlo," burbled the Irishman. "In fac'—he's on TV right now!"

They crowded into the big room. The television screen showed a distinguished, silver-haired gentleman glowering angrily at the camera. Beside him there stood a beefy individual with a half-smoked cigar clamped in one corner of his mouth, whom all instantly recognized as the chief of Knickerbocker City's police force.

The voice of an announcer off-camera came to them as they approached the set.

". . . Revealed today to be unnatural—not a genuine earthquake at all, it seems, but an artificial one, manufactured in some manner not yet known by the unknown maniac who labels himself 'the Earth-Shaker.'" The announcer's voice was shaking with tension and excitement as he continued:

"And now that Mr. Wentworth Blair has voluntarily come forward, it is learned that yet another bank in our city has been similarly threatened by this unknown criminal, and that is the highly respected State Fidelity Trust Company, one of Knickerbocker City's oldest banking establishments, founded in 1809 by . . ."

Zarkon leaned closer, his bronzed face tight, his magnetic black eyes sparkling with attentiveness.

". . . threatens, at midnight tonight, to level the State Fidelity Trust Company with another of these man-made earthquakes, unless the sum of one million dollars. . . ."

Zarkon whipped around. He snapped: "Menlo, we will need several of the equipment cases! Nick, contact the head geologist at the University—his name is Patrickson. I need to borrow his portable electronic seismographs, several of them!"

"Oboyoboyoboy!" burbled Scorchy, ecstatic, as always, when some excitement was about to happen. "What's the plan, Chief?"

Zarkon's face was grim, his voice solemn, as he answered the Irishman's query.

"The Fidelity may or may not be leveled by an earthquake at midnight," he said broodingly. "But if it is, I intend to be on the scene—"

A telephone was ringing in one of the other rooms; Miss Phoenicia Mulligan, anxious to make herself useful so she could share in the fun, scampered off to answer it. A few moments later, she returned, eyes flashing with pent-up excitement.

"That was your broker friend, Rutledge Mann, on the phone," the golden-haired girl breathed. "He said to tell you that five other banks in the city have simultaneously received threatening letters from the Earth-Shaker, each demanding one million dollars, or threatening to level the bank with an earthquake!"

They stared at her blankly.

"And each of the notes warned the bank managers to watch what happens to the Fidelity Trust at midnight tonight!" the girl finished triumphantly.

Menlo Parker suppressed a groan and turned a woeful gaze on Prince Zarkon.

"Boy, Chief, I tell you: If the Earth-Shaker really *does* bring the Fidelity down around Blair's ears tonight, by tomorrow morning there's not a bank in the city that would risk the same by refusing to pay the million!"

Zarkon said nothing, but his brow was furrowed with concern. For a criminal madman to successfully extort millions and millions of dollars through his nefarious threats was bad enough, a serious blow to the regime of law and order which Zarkon and the Omega men were all sworn to uphold.

But even worse, the loss of those millions would throw Wall Street into a chaos and the banking community into virtual collapse.

"It must not be allowed to happen," said the Omega Man in level tones, his face like flint. "Ace, get the van."

Just then, Zarkon's Hindu servant, Chandra Lal, entered the room in his quiet, deferential way, to announce that dinner was served. The stiff Rajput was seriously affronted to learn that nobody was going to be on the premises to enjoy the meal, and stalked off in a huff, hissing Hindustani curses between pinched lips.

Scorchy chuckled grimly to himself: Maybe the Earth-Shaker didn't know, but he had just made a fierce enemy of the proud Rajput. And, remembering the long knife which Chandra Lal always carried about his person, and knowing with what skill the Hindu could use the blade, the feisty little Irishman was glad not to be wearing the boots of the Earth-Shaker!

CHAPTER 8

The Earth-Shaker Strikes!

Night fell over Knickerbocker City. A thick layer of clouds obscured the moon and hid the stars behind a gloomy blanket. An ominous silence reigned in the dark streets, where inky shadows pooled between the wan glimmer of infrequent streetlights. A damp, uneasy wind prowled the lonely streets, rustling papers in the gutter and spooking an alley cat out for its evening stroll.

Joey Weston shivered as the sharp breeze cut through his turtleneck sweater, which had more than a few holes in it. But the game little newsboy did not desert his street-corner post; he tugged the bill of his wool cap down over his eyes and hugged himself for warmth through the cheap sweater. The distributor of the *Gazette* wanted his newsboys to hawk their papers until 1 A.M., and not a moment before.

Peering up at the huge illuminated clockface on its tower above the State Fidelity Trust Company, Joey saw that it was a quarter to twelve, which meant he had to stand on his chilly corner another hour and a quarter before he could take the subway home. . . .

Why his boss, Mr. Halloran, wanted his boys to work these streets when they were as deserted as Herkimer Street was at this hour was a mystery to the freckle-faced youngster. But you don't risk a decent job by asking dumb questions, the boy reasoned to himself.

The sound of a motor came to his ears. Looking around, Joey Weston saw a blue van approaching down the street. As it came up to where he stood, the boy fanned his papers automatically, but the driver, a bald Chinaman, paid him no attention beyond a quick, wary glance.

"Wuxtry! Wuxtry! Read-all-about-it!" the boy called after the retreating vehicle. "Madman Threatens Bank with Earthquake . . . aw, heck!" His voice trailed away as the blue van turned a corner and vanished from his sight. Disgustedly, the lad kicked an empty beer can lying in the gutter. It made a hollow, metallic clatter as it rolled a little ways off.

A few moments later, Joey was rather surprised to see the blue van make a reappearance around the corner, coming from the opposite direction. It pulled up across the street from the State Fidelity Trust and parked a little ways down the street, in the deeper shadows.

"Now, what the heck are you doin', mister?" the boy wondered to himself. "What'd you do, drive around the whole block?"

The headlights died. The van was dark and silent. But the newsboy noticed that the driver did not leave his vehicle, but remained in the front seat.

"Heck, maybe I can sell ya a paper, after all!" muttered the boy, and he crossed the street to come up behind the van.

Even as he did so, the big clock atop the bank's tower began to peal the hour of twelve. . . .

Peering inside the darkened van, Joey called out: "Paper, mister?"

The Chinaman behind the wheel turned a startled, vicious face upon the boy but said nothing. Cradled on his knees was a smooth box of black metal; small indicator lights glowed on its top surface, gleaming red and green. In one hand, the Oriental held a big, old-fashioned stopwatch, like those horse trainers use at racetracks to time their horses with.

"What you got there, mister?" the boy started to ask, but just then the ground shuddered underfoot, so that the lad staggered and almost fell. He dropped his papers and clung for support to the door handle.

"Gollywhoppers! *A quake!*" Joey shrilled breathlessly.

A black crack opened in the tarred surface of the street. Even as the startled boy watched wide-eyed, the crack zigzagged across the pavement in the direction of the bank.

A moment later, with a sound like rolling thunder coming nearer, Joey saw the surface of the bank *ripple* uncannily. Bricks popped out; mortar exploded in all directions. With an ear-shattering screech, the tall, tapering clock tower began to buckle and sag to one side.

"GOLLYWHOPPERS!" yelled Joey Weston.

And just then, two things happened at the same time:

The entire front of the State Fidelity Trust Company caved in with a roar of collapsing masonry like the end of the world.

And directly in front of the parked van, a manhole cover slid aside and two men jumped out onto the street and sprinted toward the blue vehicle, waving drawn guns of peculiar design. One of them was a snub-nosed little Irishman, with hair as brick red as Joey's own, and as imposing an array of freckles. The other was a long-legged, long-jawed fellow, with the blue-black, waxed and pointed beard and narrow mustachios of a stage magician.

"G-golly—" breathed Joey Weston.

As the two men charged down on the van, the door on the driver's side opened suddenly, and strong hands darted out to grab the boy's wrist and to cruelly twist it into the small of his back.

"Hey—ow! Leggo, you big lug—yer breaking my arm!" yelled the newsboy.

The Chinese lifted his other hand into view, and Joey's brave heart sank into his sneakers. For it was holding a wicked black Luger pistol, and the ice-cold mouth of the barrel pressed gougingly into the side of Joey's head.

The Irishman with the red hair stopped short at this sight.

"Stand back—both of you! Put down your weapons," hissed the Oriental in a venomous voice.

Reluctantly, Scorchy Muldoon and Nick Naldini—for, of course, it was the two Omega men—dropped their pistols.

Dragging the protesting newsboy into the van and closing the door, the Oriental gunned the vehicle to life, and it sped crazily off down the street, leaving the two comrades to stare after it grimly.

"It *was* Ching, wasn't it?" said Naldini hoarsely to his pint-sized companion.

"It was Ching," said Scorchy glumly. Then, grinding his white teeth, he added huskily: "Sure hope he doesn't hurt that kid!"

CHAPTER 9

On the Trail

As Scorchy Muldoon and Nick Naldini stood staring worriedly after the speeding van, others of the Omega crew came popping up out of their hiding places. Doc Jenkins lumbered out of the mouth of the alley, cursing glumly; Prince Zarkon had been stationed on a rooftop across the street from the State Fidelity Trust, and now came down the fire-escape ladders to join his lieutenants; Menlo Parker came out of the shadowy doorway which had effectively concealed his skinny frame. And just a few minutes later, summoned by Zarkon's pocket radio, Ace Harrigan pulled up behind the wheel of the equipment van, which had been parked a couple of blocks away. They all knew there was no point in trying to chase after the blue van, which had long since vanished and by now was thoroughly lost in the maze of streets.

"Let's collect our seismograph readings and get back to headquarters," suggested Zarkon quietly. He and Menlo had attached a dozen small but highly sensitive instruments in a broad circle around the block on which the demolished bank had stood. While Menlo supervised the detaching of the seismographs, which had been borrowed from the University, Zarkon called the police, ambulances and fire trucks to the scene. As no one had been in the bank, and as the police had, earlier in the evening, unobtrusively cleared out all of the tenants from the adjoining buildings, there was no need for the ambulances, and they departed from the scene.

"Sure hope Ching don't hurt that kid!" muttered the peppery little prizefighter in anxious tones.

Zarkon bade him calm his fears. "Probably the van's driver merely snatched the boy as a hostage," he said. "Once well away from the possibility of pursuit, he doubtless let him go. Let us hope so, anyway."

With his night binoculars, Zarkon had easily read the license number on the blue van, which he reported to the police. Within mere minutes, the License Bureau reported the plates as having been stolen that afternoon from an automobile parked on a side street in Long Island.

"Another false lead, dangitall!" cussed Scorchy gloomily.

The Omega men and the cops discussed the incident in low tones, regretfully. Zarkon did not contribute to the conversation. He was feeling guilty, for had he not intervened, the entire area would have been cordoned off and none of this would have happened. Zarkon had felt confident that he and his lieutenants would have been able to immobilize the blue van before it escaped . . . but the presence of the newsboy, a factor that could not have been foretold, effectively ruined all of their plans.

"When the morning dailies hit the street," prophesied Doc Jenkins glumly, "the financial world will be frothing at the mouth! It's gonna be touch and go t' keep them other banks from givin' in to Earth-Shaker's demands."

"Yes, but somehow it must be done," said Zarkon firmly. "The metropolis cannot permit itself to meekly surrender to the extortionate demands of the criminal element, no matter how clever."

Menlo came up to where they stood, huffing and wheezing. "Got 'em all, Chief," he reported, indicating the seismograph rolls. "Let's get back to headquarters and check 'em over!"

Ace Harrigan drove them back in the equipment van.

It was going to be a long night. . . .

The blue van whipped into side streets, turned down alleys, and before it had gone more than a dozen blocks from the scene on Herkimer Street, Ching realized that he had evaded all pursuit and could safely relax.

He pulled up under a streetlight and roughly thrust the newsboy from the cab. The lad sprawled to the sidewalk and came scrambling to his feet, shaking his small but sturdy fist after the vehicle as it drove away.

"C'mon back an' fight, ya big bully!" the boy squalled. Then he looked around rapidly, recognizing the neighborhood in which the Eurasian had dumped him. He was in a poor area filled with cheap rooming houses and run-down tenements, he knew.

He also realized, with a little surge of excitement, that one of his school chums, a newsboy like himself, called Freddy Freeman, lived not far away. Joey Weston took to his heels. The handsome, dark-haired lad had a bad leg, but he was keeping another boy's bicycle for him at the moment, Joey knew. The crippled newsboy couldn't ride the bike himself but never minded doing favors for a friend.

Joey had a hunch he could borrow the bike from Freddy Freeman, and a bike was what he needed, for wheels are a lot faster than legs. And Joey firmly determined to follow the escaping blue van before it got far enough away to lose itself in the labyrinthine streets of Knickerbocker City.

Joey Weston, it happened, idolized the Omega men and knew them all from their pictures in the papers. For, while they seldom permitted themselves to be photographed, Prince Zarkon and the Omega men had in the past turned up on the front pages of the tabloids in connection with this or that sensational crime-solving feat.

And despite his anger, excitement and fear, Joey had instantly recognized Scorchy Muldoon and Nick Naldini when they had popped up from the manhole to charge the blue van.

Telling his crippled chum that he was working with the Omega men on the Earth-Shaker case, he succeeded in borrowing the bike and went zooming off down the street, peddling furiously. At this early hour in the morning there was hardly any traffic on this side of town, just an occasional cruising taxi or a bread truck making its morning deliveries.

As he bicycled in speedy pursuit of the van, Joey's mind raced, rapidly rehearsing the streets of this area and trying to guess where the van might turn off and where it could not turn, because of one-way-traffic signs. Surely, he had a chance to spot the vehicle; there was at least a chance.

That Joey Weston was able to catch sight of the blue van marked JOE'S DIAPER SERVICE was due to several factors: The boy's own quick thinking in borrowing the bike and the rapidity of his pursuit were one, of course. But, also, the Chinaman behind the wheel of the fleeing van: The last thing Ching wanted was to attract the attention of a traffic cop by running a red light or by speeding, so he drove off, after dumping the newsboy, at a moderate speed, scrupulously observing the traffic laws.

When Joey spotted the van far down the all-but-deserted street, the boy's heart raced excitedly. "Hot dog!" he ejaculated, tingling all over with the thrill of the chase. And then he slowed his speed, so as not to make himself an object of attention in the rearview mirror.

The brave newsboy followed the van as it wove a circuitous route through the nighted streets and approached the waterfront. There, ramshackle tenements gave way to gloomy, unlit warehouses and storage buildings, with the occasional gaudy flicker of a defective neon sign denoting an all-night diner or a seedy tavern.

The van slowed as it approached the huge doors of one such warehouse. The headlights dimmed, then brightened, then dimmed again, in what was obviously a prearranged signal.

The doors swung open with a creaking of rusty hinges. The van nosed into the darkness of the warehouse, and the doors closed behind it.

Joey pedaled around the corner, out of sight of anyone who might be watching from one of the upper windows of the warehouse, and found the nearest street-corner phone booth. Hopping off the borrowed bike, the boy called Information, got the number of Omega, and hung up to dial again.

The telephone box, however, refused to disgorge his dime, although the lad impatiently jiggled the return switch.

"Oh, gollywhoppers!" the boy said disgustedly, digging into his pockets to find another dime.

Then his heart sank in his chest.

With growing dismay, Joey Weston turned out each of his pockets and discovered that he did not have another dime.

Back at Omega, Fooey Mulligan had been watching the news on the big television set in the main room. As the five Omega men and their leader came tramping disheartenedly into the room, she turned to survey them with a distinctly *un*ladylike sneer on her handsome features.

"I see you birds blew it again," the blond girl chortled. "Serves you right, smarties! Now, if you'd've let *me* go along, maybe things would have turned out neater. . . ."

"Aw, c'mon, Fooey," groaned Scorchy gloomily. "We feel lousy enough, without you tossing yer two cents in."

Menlo and Zarkon vanished into the laboratory to scrutinize the seismograph readings, while the others flopped down on the sofas to watch an excited newscaster recapitulating the tale of the second disaster.

". . . only that, in the case of the State Fidelity Trust Company disaster, it was accompanied by no known loss of life," he was babbling away at high speed. "Meanwhile, in Palma Laguna, California, scientists at the Richter Institute told members of the press that an earthquake along the East Coast is an anomaly, if not an actual scientific impossibility. Questioned by a reporter from our WNX-TV affiliate in Palma Laguna, Professor Waldo F. Perkins further explained—"

"Aw, turn it off, Doc," sighed Scorchy grumpily. "I'm gonna ring fer Chandra Lal, see if he can rustle up some grub. I heard enough o' that guff!"

But there proved to be no need for him to do so, as the tall Hindu servant at that moment materialized from the kitchen with a silver tray loaded with dishes of food.

CHAPTER 10

Mystery Mummy

Ching drove the blue van up the ramp and into the dark and cavernous interior of the seemingly-abandoned warehouse and parked it. He emerged from the cab, carrying with him the black box and stopwatch, and stood for a moment, narrowly watching as a crew of tough-looking men in gray coveralls checked every inch of the vehicle with instruments to see if one or another of the Omega men had managed to plant a radio "bug" anywhere on the machine.

"All clean, sir," one of the workmen reported. The other nodded with a curt word, and turned away. Entering a steel door, he descended to the subbasement level by means of a high-speed pneumatic elevator and approached huge, heavy, ponderous metal doors such as those which guard bank vaults.

Ching touched a button in the wall beside the massive steel frame, and a moment later he was uncomfortably aware of the silent scrutiny of hidden television cameras which recorded his identity and the fact that he was alone and unaccompanied.

With a husky wheeze of compressed air, the enormously heavy steel doors swung open on oiled gimbals. He stepped into a brilliantly lit cubicle, and the doors swung smoothly shut behind him.

Placing the black box and the stopwatch in a locker, Ching rapidly undressed, removing every last stitch of clothing. Then he donned protective goggles and thumbed a switch. A buzzing sound came to his ears, and his bare skin tingled eerily as his naked body was bathed in the invisible rays of a powerful projector of ultraviolet light.

As soon as the UV lamp had turned itself off, the Chinaman opened an airtight canister and withdrew a one-piece, sterile garment of gleaming white metallic fabric. This he donned before touching another button in the wall. An airtight door slid open noiselessly, and he stepped into a room like an operating theater.

The walls were of immaculately clean, snow-white tile and scrubbed, glistening metal. Brilliant neon tubes cast an unwavering light upon the fantastic figure that sat facing him in a wheelchair, accompanied by a white-masked medical attendant and a naked black giant.

Ching bowed humbly before the figure seated in the wheelchair and stood a trifle nervously as he was subjected to the scrutiny of unseen eyes.

The man was tall and powerfully built, with a bullethead either naturally bald or shaven bare. Most of his face and body were swathed in sterile white bandages, and his eyes were hidden behind opaque goggles.

Between the interstices in the mummy-like wrappings could be seen hideously scarred areas of flesh. It was as if the man in the chair had not very long since been terribly burned in a conflagration. But here and there, similar interstices revealed areas of pink, healthy flesh, where skin grafts had been successful.

In a deep, controlled voice, the figure in the mummy wrappings addressed the Oriental. "Your report?" the voice demanded tonelessly.

Ching bowed again. "Master, the State Fidelity Trust Company building has been totally destroyed according to schedule."

The bandaged man nodded in satisfaction. "The police, then, had not cordoned off the area? There was no blockade of the streets?"

"No, Master," murmured Ching in his sibilant voice, which lingered with a little hissing intonation over the aspirates. "At least two of the Omega men were concealed under a manhole in the street, but I took hostage a small boy who chanced to be on the scene, and escaped without exchanging a shot."

"Very good! I trust there was no effort at pursuit?"

Ching indicated that there had not been.

"And your hostage? How did you dispose of the child?" inquired the mummy-like figure.

Ching shrugged, perspiring a little under the brilliant lights. "As soon as I had left the immediate vicinity of the bank and had ascertained to my satisfaction that the van was not being pursued, I forced him out of the cab and left him on the street," he explained.

"Hm," frowned the bald man. "That was perhaps unwise of you, Ching. The boy will be able to identify you, and the van as well . . . you should have disposed of him in a manner more permanent."

"Master," protested Ching smoothly, "both of the Omega men saw and recognized me, and, anyway, is it not time that we altered the appearance of the van, now that it has been twice seen?"

"Perhaps you are right. Very well; that is all."

Ching bowed again and left the immaculate room, leaving the bandage-swathed figure seated motionlessly under the blazing lights.

In the sterilization cubicle, he again changed his garments, donning the clothing he had earlier worn.

As soon as he felt the ponderous steel doors close behind him, Ching released a shaky, long-pent breath. Reaching into his pocket, he removed therefrom a flat white-and-gold box. He extracted a cigarette and lit it with a match.

It was a gold-tipped Dimitrio.

Dawn was pale in the east when Zarkon and Menlo completed their work with the seismograph recordings and called the Omega men into the laboratory. They were followed by Miss Phoenicia Mulligan, who had fallen asleep curled up on one of the sofas and was yawning and stretching sleepily.

"You boys sure keep crummy hours!" the blond girl observed grouchily. No one bothered to answer her jibe.

"Ace," said Zarkon, turning to the tall aviator, "will you contact William Harper Littlejohn and set up an appointment for me to meet with him this morning? Menlo and I have studied the seismograph readings, but I want the opinion of a veteran geologist before proceeding further in that direction."

"Sure, Chief," grinned the airman.

"Find out anything interesting, Chief?" inquired Doc Jenkins in his heavy, slow voice. The Man from Tomorrow nodded.

"I think so. . . . Menlo, pull down the chart, will you?"

The scrawny scientist pulled down a huge wall chart which displayed a minutely detailed, block-by-block map of Knickerbocker City and its suburbs and environs. Over this, Prince Zarkon affixed a sheet of transparent plastic, fastening it into place with tape. Then he removed colored grease pencils from a box on the lab stand.

He marked the overlay sheet carefully, then stood back.

"The red squares represent the two banks the Earth-Shaker has already destroyed," he said somberly. "And the black squares stand for the other banks he has thus far threatened with destruction. Now . . . do you notice anything peculiar about the disposition of the markings I have made?"

They studied the wall chart thoughtfully. Then Scorchy Muldoon spoke up with puzzlement in his tones. "Yeah, Chief . . . them two marks there line up almost eggzac'ly east t' west!"

"And so do these two down here," murmured Phoenicia Mulligan interestedly.

"But what does it mean, Chief?" asked Nick Naldini.

Zarkon shrugged slightly. "Perhaps nothing at all; but perhaps it may be of significance. If the earthquakes are of natural origin, buildings will be damaged along fault lines, which, due to the crystalline structure of the bedrock under Knickerbocker City, *should* run in geometrically straight lines—"

"And since them two up there line up, and them two down there do too, you think th' quakes are natural?" asked Muldoon, scratching his fiery-thatched head.

Zarkon nodded—reluctantly.

"But, Holy Houdini, Chief!" protested Nick Naldini, waving his hands. "Natural earthquakes don't happen on previously announced schedules, do they? How can this Earth-Shaker guy know just when they're gonna happen, and which buildings they're gonna destroy?"

"Good thinking, Nick," said Prince Zarkon. "If they are of purely natural origin, he could not. Therefore, they must have been triggered off by some artificial cause. The question is: By what cause?"

"Bombs," said Phoenicia succinctly. But Zarkon shook his head.

"As much as I would enjoy agreeing with you, Phoenicia," said the Nemesis of Evil, "the seismograph readings indicate otherwise. I will feel more certain about this, once I have had a chance to talk the matter over with Dr. Littlejohn and show him the readings."

"Well, if not by bombs, then by what?" demanded the blond heiress practically.

"That remains to be discovered," said Zarkon grimly.

Then he added: "Ace, make that call to Littlejohn now, if you please."

CHAPTER 11

The Mystery Deepens

Joey stood shivering on the street corner, wondering what to do. The eastern sky was beginning to glow with dawn, and the cold, wet wind from the river was whistling through his ragged sweater. He was so near the river that he could hear the waves sloshing and slapping against the sides of the pier on which the warehouse was built.

The plucky newsboy didn't dare leave the scene, lest the blue van drive away. But, without a coin in his pockets, he couldn't even call the police, much less the headquarters of the Omega men.

He thought briefly about retracing his steps and trying to bum a dime from a waitress in that all-night diner he had bicycled past, but gave it up as a punk idea. He didn't dare leave the vicinity of the warehouse until he was certain that help was on the way.

"Gollywhoppers!" the lad grumbled to himself in aggrieved tones. "Sure wish Mr. Halloran hadn't come by when he did: I'd a had plenty of change left over by now!" The newboy's boss regularly drove around the streets about midnight to collect the earnings of his crew, in order to prevent their getting mugged on the way home and losing their earnings. And last night he had driven by a trifle earlier than usual. Which had left the Weston boy with nothing in his jeans but a subway token, his return fare home.

Suddenly the boy jumped, and his freckled face split into a wide grin. A moment later, he puckered up his face in a frown of self-disgust.

"Boy, am I a dumbo!" he breathed. For something had just occurred to him that had slipped from his recollection in the urgency and excitement of chasing the bank-busters.

That was that from a street-corner telephone box, anywhere in Knickerbocker City, you can place an emergency call to the authorities without having a coin in your possession, simply by dialing the operator.

He did so now, and waited, tapping his fingers impatiently against the side of the instrument while the phone rang and rang. Eventually, a bored, tired voice said: "Operator?"

"Operator, I wanna place an emergency call to Omega in the city —I dunno their number," he said rapidly into the receiver.

There was a moment's silence.

"Are you certain that this is an emergency call, sir?" inquired the voice at the other end, sounding suspicious. Joey assured the operator that it was. Moments later, he heard the phone at the other end ring, and somebody picked it up.

"Omega," said a voice.

"My name's Joey Weston—Joseph Randolph Weston, Jr., that is," he said hurriedly. "I'm a newsboy, working on Herkimer Street. I saw the bank bein' wrecked last night, and I foll—"

"Begorra, jus' hold on a minute!" exclaimed the voice at the other end. "Are you the kid the van snatched?"

"Yessir!" breathed Joey. Then he added, "Mr. Muldoon, sir!" for he guessed the identity of his interrogator from the lilt of the Emerald Isle in his excited voice.

"Cheez! You ain't hurt or nuthin'!" anxiously demanded Scorchy Muldoon.

Joey grinned. "Naw, that guy never laid a mitt on me!" he said, a trifle inaccurately. "He lemme go a dozen blocks away. I grabbed—"

"Chinaman, was it? Thick-lensed glasses?"

"Yep! I mean: Yessir, Mr. Muldoon."

"How'd'ya know me name's Muldoon?" demanded the Irishman suspiciously. "This ain't no crank call, is it?"

"Nossir!" declared the newsboy staunchly. Then he quickly explained how he had recognized Scorchy Muldoon and Nick Naldini from their newspaper pictures, when they jumped out of the sewer manhole to confront the blue van.

". . . I grabbed a pal's bike and scooted after 'im," the lad confided in breathless tones. "I followed the van all the way to this warehouse on . . ."

Joey had a sharp eye and a clear memory, and accurately reported the street number and name stenciled on the wooden sign above the entrance to the seemingly abandoned warehouse.

"Okay, sonny—good work!" approved the pugilist warmly. "We'll be there right away—in the meanwhile, now, I don't wantcha to get in any more trouble, unnerstan'? You lay low. Just keep an eye on the place. Promise?"

"I promise, Mr. Muldoon, sir," said Joey Weston solemnly. Then he hung up the phone and leaned against the side of the booth, dizzy with excitement and suspense.

Boy, just wait till the gang heard about this—how he helped Prince Zarkon and the Omega men trap the bank-threatener!

Scorchy hung up the phone and called the others to his side, repeating the account the plucky little newsboy had reported to him on the telephone.

Doc Jenkins frowned, looked blank-eyed for a moment while he consulted his computer-like memory, which was stuffed and stocked with an endless number of apparently unimportant facts and data. Then he spoke up to say that, according to the latest listings from the Municipal Tax Assessor's Office (as reported in the *Daily Sentinel*), that particular warehouse had been empty and abandoned for seven months, ever since the owner, the Caribbean-American Fruit Company, had gone out of business.

"Sure the kid's on the up-an'-up, Scorchy?" he inquired dubiously. "Sounds like a nut call to me. Why'd the van drive inside an empty warehouse, anyway?"

"The kid sounded straight enough to me," snapped Scorchy in return. "And why wouldn't the van park in a warehouse? They gotta know the cops are lookin' for it all over town by now—so they gotta hide it *some*where."

Doc Jenkins shrugged. "Well . . . mebbe so, mebbe not," said the big man philosophically. "Wish the Chief wuz here: *He'd* know what to do about it!"

"The Chief'd do just what Scorchy wants to do: check it out," argued Nick Naldini. "If it's a crank call, what harm to look into it?"

Doc Jenkins did a double-take, regarding the saturnine stage wizard with slack-jawed astonishment. Even Scorchy looked stupefied. And Phoenicia Mulligan shook her head numbly as if to dislodge the cobwebs and start the thinking mechanism up again.

"What's eatin' you birds?" demanded Naldini hotly.

Fooey laughed. "Nothing much," she said with cool amusement. "It's just the first time in recorded history that you and Scorchy ever agreed on anything, that's all!"

"C'mon, Nick, let's go," said the pint-sized pugilist with a lofty expression on his freckled mug. "We'll show these doubtin' Thomases—"

"Be sure you call the Chief on the car phone," Doc called after them, "and let him know what's up." Zarkon had already departed with Ace Harrigan for his early-morning conference with William Harper Littlejohn.

They promised to do so, took their gear, and went to the underground garage to select a vehicle for the trip.

"*I'll* drive, Small Change," sneered Nick Naldini, reverting to form after his momentary lapse from their old and interminable feud.

"Oh, yeah?" demanded Scorchy. "Whyzat?" The feisty little Irishman heartily resented any slurs on his abilities behind the wheel, and sensed one coming up. Nor was he mistaken.

"Because I want to get there in one piece, is all!" retorted the vaudevillian with a sneer.

Scorchy flushed until the tips of his ears were as scarlet as his tousled locks. "Why, you two-bit bottom-of-the-bill stage ham! Faith, and I'll tie yer skinny legs inta a pretzel—!" he blustered.

"You and what squad of commandos, Half Pint?" snarled Naldini.

They drove out of the underground parking space, still quarreling violently, and vanished down the street.

Zarkon arrived at the entrance of one of the most famous and imposing of the skyscrapers in Knickerbocker City and took the private elevator to the eighty-sixth floor. Entering the reception room, he found Littlejohn in a bathrobe, yawning sleepily and awaiting his arrival.

"Sorry to disturb your rest by coming at so early an hour," said the Nemesis of Evil, "but affairs are pressing and time is of the essence. I would like your professional opinion on these readings."

He spread the seismograph records out on a long table. Adjusting his monocle in one eye, Johnny studied them closely. "I'll be superamalgamated!" the older man breathed faintly.

"Something interesting?" Zarkon inquired.

Littlejohn continued scrutinizing the seismograph recordings. "How many instruments had you placed . . . and at what distance from the epicenter?" he inquired. The Prince told him.

Johnny looked flabbergasted.

"What is the matter?"

"An indubitable malfunction of hypernormality, which—" Johnny Littlejohn overcame his innate penchant for big words with an almost physical effort. Controlling himself, he continued: "Explosives, planted deeply enough, can set off what appears to be a natural earthquake," he said tensely. "However, in such cases, the seismic readings are unmistakable. The initial blast registers the highest, and the tremors subside from that point on. Whereas, in natural earthquakes, the tremors build towards a peak, then taper off rapidly."

"And this means?"

Johnny gestured at the readings. "See for yourself! The readings conform in every detail to those recorded by natural earthquakes."

CHAPTER 12

Joey Gets in Trouble

Joey hung around the street corner, taking an occasional surreptitious peek to see if the garage doors had opened and the van had been moved since his last look, but all remained normal and quiet. The seemingly-abandoned warehouse showed no lights or activity whatsoever.

"Gollywhoppers, I wish they'd get here!" the newsboy breathed to himself, shivering in his ragged sweater and hugging his arms against his ribs to warm himself. Dawn was peeping up above the rooftops, and the morning breeze blew cold and damp from the river, which sloshed and gurgled against the concrete pilings.

It seemed unnatural to the lad that no lights showed in the windows of the rickety old building, and after a time Joey began to wonder if there were any sounds coming from within. Taking a chance, the lad scuttled across the street and inched along the front of the warehouse, keeping well out of sight of any person who might be watching.

The front windows were boarded up, and no light showed through the chinks between the boards. But, around to one side, where a narrow wooden platform like an old-fashioned front porch ran the length of the wall, filling the space between the side of the building and the edge of the pier on which it was built, he found unboarded windows. They were grimy with dust and hard to see through, but what he saw gave Joey a little thrill of excitement and alarm.

A vast, cavernous interior revealed itself dimly by the light of shaded lamps. He saw a cement floor, stained and splotched with oil. The blue van with its sign, JOE'S DIAPER SERVICE, clearly legible, was parked in the middle of the cement floor, and a half dozen men in overalls were working around the vehicle.

They were spray-painting it a different color.

"Gollywhoppers!" the boy said to himself, standing on tiptoes to observe the scene.

They had masked the windshield and side windows with pieces of thick absorbent paper tacked in place with gummed tape and were wielding spray guns. Joey could just faintly hear the hiss of compressed air as the paint was sprayed on the van.

But . . . *what color* were they repainting the vehicle? Through the grimy window, Joey couldn't make the color out. It was something dark and nondescript.

Two other men, on the side facing Joey's position, were changing the sign painted on the side of the van. They were using cardboard stencils which covered the original lettering now painted over, but what the new inscription read was another thing that Joey could not tell, since they were in the way.

Joey instantly realized, with a little thrill of alarm, that before very long, when the quick-drying paint had dried and the new sign had been lettered on the side, the malefactors could safely drive the van through the streets of Knickerbocker City without attracting any attention at all.

The cops, and the Omega men, were looking for a dark blue van with JOE'S DIAPER SERVICE written on the sides. They were most definitely *not* looking for a green or gray or black van marked with different lettering.

The Omega men had not, as yet, arrived on the scene. So it was up to Joey to ascertain the new appearance of the van, so he could pass the word along.

But . . . how?

The newsboy prowled the length of the building, examining each window in turn. One or two of the windows had been broken and were stoutly boarded up, but all the unbroken ones were locked tightly.

"If I bust one of these windows in," the boy muttered to himself, trying to figure out what to do, "it may make enough noise for those guys to hear me, even above the noise of sprayin'. An' *that* wouldn't be smart!"

In the rear of the building, however, Joey found one window propped partly open, probably for ventilation. He squirmed over the ledge, as quietly as he possibly could, and dropped lightly to the cement floor, his worn sneakers making hardly any sound. Across the length of the warehouse, he could see the men working on the van under the glare of the shaded lights, and began worming his way nearer to where they were, keeping in the shadows and ducking behind the posts which supported the upper storey whenever one of them happened to turn in his direction.

When he was close enough to make the scene out, Joey crouched behind an empty packing crate and took a good, long look.

They were painting the van a dull black, he now saw, and the sign they were lettering over the old sign read BONJOUR FLO-RISTS. *That* was important news for him to give the Omega men.

With a slight twinge of guilt, Joey Weston remembered the promise he had given Scorchy Muldoon about staying away from the warehouse and keeping out of trouble.

"I better get outa here," the boy breathed to himself, and turned away. Creeping between two empty packing crates, he headed for the rear of the huge room, where one open window gave forth on a view of the river.

But some one of the workmen had carelessly left an empty gallon paint can between the crates, and Joey failed to see it in the gloom of the dark, cavernous interior. He knocked it over with a hollow clatter that seemed startlingly loud to the scared boy—almost as loud as the sound of his heart thudding against his ribs.

One of the workmen ambled over to investigate, growling something about "doggone rats." He found the boy crouched on his heels, voiced an exclamation, and hauled the boy to his feet with a firm grip on the scruff of his neck.

"Look what I found, boss!" called the workman, dragging the newsboy out into the glare of the lights.

His heart sinking into his heels, Joey Weston looked up into the cold, impassive and inscrutable features of the sinister oriental man who had been driving the van earlier. It was the same man who had held the muzzle of the pistol against Joey's head and had carried him off in the flight from the Omega men.

"Ssso," murmured Ching softly. When he was tense or excited, his voice tended to linger over s's a bit. "And what have you there, Louie? It would seem that there is a sspy in our midst. . . ."

Bright and early that morning, the Mayor of Knickerbocker City awoke to find the metropolis in an uproar over the Earth-Shaker. He had scheduled a full-sized news conference for nine o'clock in the morning, and waddled into the crowded room to face a battery of cameras and a barrage of hysterical questions.

"Dagnabit," groaned the Mayor under his breath as he shoved his way through the crowd of reporters. Mayor Phineas T. Bulver was a bit of a novelty to Knickerbocker City's citizenry, a real old-fashioned small-town politician who had gotten himself the biggest job in the biggest city on the coast. A short, stout, red-faced man, with a bald brow and an excitable way of talking, he was already a favorite with the reporters, who knew by now that they could always count on him for a juicy quote or a blistering headline when the news was dull.

The people of Knickerbocker City liked him too. He was a refreshing change after a succession of smooth-talking, college-educated, upper-crust mayors, or slab-sided machine politicians. They enjoyed his candor, his cussing, and his blunt honesty, for Phineas T. Bulver never shied away from calling a spade a spade. "All right, all right, dagnabit, boys," he yelled above the hubbub, waving his hands for attention. "If you'll just hesh up so you can hear me. . . ."

Together with the Mayor were a number of portly, distinguished-looking men in expensive business suits. These were representatives of the Stock Exchange and the banking community of the city: In particular, they were the directors of the banking institutions which the Earth-Shaker had singled out to receive his ransom demands.

In a firm voice, the Mayor read a prepared statement which had taken him most of the night to write. He deplored the destruction of the State Fidelity Trust Company's building, praised the police and firemen for their prompt, efficient work in reducing the calamity to an irreducible minimum, and exhorted the people of Knickerbocker City not to yield to panic. In particular, he addressed himself to the members of the banking community, to their investors, and to their depositors.

"We do not yet know whether these two disasters were actually caused by the criminal maniac who calls himself 'the Earth-Shaker,'" he said, "or whether he somehow had foreknowledge of the earthquakes and decided to capitalize on that knowledge."

"Mr. Mayor!" called one of the television newsmen. "When you say 'caused,' does that imply that you believe it's possible for this crook to somehow have triggered an earthquake?"

The Mayor spread his hands for silence. "The top officials of our police department and detective bureaus," he replied, "working in close association with leading scientists from the University, are investigating that subject at this very moment, and it would be premature for me to give any opinion on the matter at this time."

"But, Mr. Mayor—"

"Now listen, boys," said the Mayor, wiping his perspiring brow on a handkerchief, "give me a break! I'm gonna read this statement if we have to sit here all day—and the oftener you interrupt me with your questions, the longer it'll take."

The reprimand was a sensible one, so the flurry of questions subsided and relative quiet reigned anew.

As soon as he had their undivided attention again, the Mayor went on to plead with the citizens of Knickerbocker City not to give way to fear or despair.

"In particular, I want to assure you that the directors of the banks being threatened by this madman are firmly resolved, as I am, not to hand over one cent to this kind of emotional blackmail," swore the Mayor. Behind him, the bankers looked nervous, reluctant, unhappy and truculent all at once. But none of them dared disagree with His Honor.

"The last thing we want is a panic on the floor of the Stock Exchange," the Mayor went on. "And it would cripple our city economically if the worried citizens rushed into their banks to withdraw all of their savings on the chance that the Earth-Shaker makes good on his latest threat. So . . . I've asked the Governor of our state to declare today a bank holiday, and no bank in this city will be open until tomorrow, at best."

This was stunning news, and the reporters blinked incredulously. The last time the Governor had closed the banks of Knickerbocker City had been during the stock-market collapse during the Great Depression.

The more quick-thinking among the reporters realized that the Mayor had let something slip, for beyond listing the names of the banks which had received the latest threat from the Earth-Shaker, no details on what particular bank was the next in line for his nefarious attentions had been given out.

"What bank is next on the list, Mr. Mayor?" queried a reporter from one of the metropolitan dailies.

"The Berkeley National Bank and Trust," replied the Mayor.

"And did the Earth-Shaker say when he was going to destroy the bank, if the director didn't pay up?"

The Mayor shook his head. "Today, at noon," he said unhappily.

CHAPTER 13

Omega to the Rescue

Scorchy and Nick pulled up around the corner from the big warehouse and parked the car, looking around. The neighborhood was deserted at this hour of the morning, only a couple of cabs were cruising for early fares, and nobody at all was on the streets.

Scorchy glanced in every direction. "Where d'ye suppose that kid's gotten to?" he demanded worriedly.

Nick Naldini shrugged. "I dunno, but that looks like his bike," the lanky stage magician drawled, pointing at the bicycle which Joey had left leaning up against the telephone booth. Scorchy checked out the number of the phone. It tallied with what the phone company had told him, back before they had driven away from headquarters. Always on the alert for crank calls, Scorchy had checked to see from which public phone Joey had placed the call to Omega. The location of the phone had been around the corner from the address of the warehouse, so everything seemed on the up-and-up.

Scorchy gave the bike a gloomy look. "Dang that kid!" he muttered sourly. "I *tol'* him to stick around and wait fer us t' come. Probably got hisself in trouble by now, if I know kids!"

"Hope not," Nick declared. Then he glanced at his pint-sized pal. "Well, what do we do now? Got any ideas, Short Stuff? There's the warehouse, and presumably the van's inside—what's your plan?"

Scorchy looked undecided. The feisty little Irishman's first impulse was to plunge into the fray, fists swinging . . . but if their young informant was perhaps being held by the crooks, this put a damper on his plan. It would never do to endanger the boy, whose determination, bravery and quick thinking had guided them to this spot.

For one thing, Zarkon severely disapproved of endangering the public in any conflict between Omega and crime.

"Dunno," the redhead confessed. "Tried t' call the Chief, but he was holed up with Johnny Littlejohn. Ace said he'd pass him the word when he came back to the car . . . dang it! Once we get them 'personal phones' we won't have this problem anymore!"

Muldoon referred to an invention that Menlo Parker was currently working on, designing a miniaturized portable radio-telephone which the Omega operatives could carry on their person at all times, and by which they could always get in touch with one another, and also tap into the public phone lines to contact the police, fire department, or ambulance. The invention was by no means yet perfected.

"Guess we just check it out," muttered Scorchy, hauling an equipment case out of the back seat. The two men set the device up between them and directed a stream of radar-like impulses toward the front of the warehouse.

Signal lights flashed on the panel of the compact instrument, and the needles of several dials jumped, indicating that the warehouse contained a sizable metal object, big enough to be a motor vehicle.

"Guess the van's still there, anyway," said Scorchy cheerfully. "Course, it might drive off at any minute . . . dang it, if we could git in, we might catch the whole blamed gang flat-footed!"

"Maybe we should call the cops," suggested Nick Naldini, but with reluctance audible in his hoarse whiskey voice. The Omega men had nothing against the police, certainly, but they vastly preferred to do things their own way, without interference. Still and all, it was probably what Zarkon would have done, had he been on the scene.

"Naw," scoffed Scorchy. "If these ginks are smart enough t' figger out how to cause earthquakes, they're smart enough to have plenty o' ways to duck outa there before the cops c'd bust in. Let's sneak up on the place and use these," he added, selecting small egg-shaped objects from the equipment case and hefting them on the palm of one hand.

Nick eyed the gas grenades dubiously. The anaesthetic vapor stored under pressure in the small, fragile containers was colorless and odorless and certainly potent enough to fell a score of unsuspecting men, but. . . .

"A typical dumb idea, Small Change," he remarked sarcastically. "Gotta bust a window to get it in, and that'll give the whole show away. Let's use the new Injector instead."

Although automatically riled at Naldini's sarcasm, the Irishman had to admit his idea was better. They opened another compartment of the case and drew forth something that looked like a Buck Rogers raygun. Opening the clip in the butt of the weapon, Naldini inserted a tube-shaped canister and clicked the device shut.

"Let's go," he drawled.

They left the car and crossed the street, strolling at an ordinary pace and pretending to make small talk, in case any eyes happened to be watching them from the upper windows of the warehouse. Pausing in front of the building, they loitered as if waiting in deep discussion, and Scorchy unobtrusively stuck the muzzle of the Injector into the narrow slit between the big garage doors.

He pulled the trigger, waited some thirty seconds, then replaced the Injector under his coat. The two strolled on to the next corner and stood waiting for the traffic light to change, although there was hardly any traffic to speak of. Nick gave the dial of his wristwatch a casual glance.

"All's clear," he announced.

They went back to the big doors and checked them out. Scorchy pointed to the windows on the front of the warehouse, which were boarded up, apparently so as to frustrate anyone who might be trying to look in from the street.

"Door's bolted from inside," he said. "Let's try one of the windows."

"Okay, but hurry up. Gas doesn't last forever, you know," Nick growled.

They kicked one of the boarded windows in and entered the huge, all-but-empty room. Before them, the van, half-repainted, sat. Ringed about it were the sprawled bodies of several men, obviously felled by the anaesthetic vapors from the gas gun.

"Bull's-eye!" chortled Scorchy Muldoon.

Nick Naldini gave a nasty grin.

The gas which the Injector had discharged into the warehouse was odorless and invisible, a concoction made by one of the formulas secret to Omega. The vapor was heavier than air and tended to settle toward the ground, which explained why it had knocked out the workmen.

They approached the half-repainted van with drawn guns, which they knew were not needed. But the Omega men did not just charge in with sheer bravado, taking chances. When and if they entered the stronghold of the enemy, it was with a good chance of survival. Like right now.

The anaesthetic gas dissipated quickly, and the effects of the gas upon the human body were relatively quickly recovered from, but one thing about the gas the Injector had filled the warehouse with, it was heavier than air and only filled the huge room to about the height of twenty feet.

The Omega men found themselves staring into the barrel of a revolver.

The gun was held by their old friend Ching, who stood upon a rickety wooden balcony which circled the room at about twenty-five feet from the floor.

Beside him, with a white, frightened face, was the little newsboy, Joey Weston.

Ching smiled silkily.

"Stand where you are and raise your hands above your heads," he ordered. "Pleasse," he added in his hissing voice.

Scorchy Muldoon and Nick Naldini exchanged a glance. They were not wearing one of the bulletproof "business suits" available in their lockers. It had not occurred to them that they should don the protective garments. Now they rather wished they had, although, actually, the revolver Ching held was pointed at their heads, rather than their torsos.

"Lay down your guns," advised Ching.

They did so.

Ching looked them over. From the fact that they were not wearing anything resembling gas masks, he presumed that the vapor they had injected into the warehouse had become harmless or had dissipated, but he knew better than to presume much of anything where Zarkon's lieutenants were concerned. He nudged the newsboy beside him.

"You will precede me down the stairs," he ordered. And Joey Weston was not about to disagree with someone who held a gun. The lad went carefully down the wooden steps, followed by Ching.

He reached the cement floor, half expecting to pass out, but as Ching had gathered, the gas had become harmless. Ching prodded him across the floor until he and his captor stood before the two Omega men. Joey eyed the two of them shamefacedly.

"I'm real sorry, Mr. Muldoon," said the lad humbly.

The redhead grinned. " 'Tis nothin', me b'y," he said heartily. "I'd a done th' same in yer shoes, prob'ly."

The newsboy smiled faintly.

Ching eyed his two captives narrowly. He, of course, knew them both on sight, having faced them before. And he believed them to be very dangerous. For the Omega men had other weapons than mere guns, and could not be given anything less than total attention.

He was sweating slightly, was Ching. For he faced two dangerous adversaries, and he knew it.

And he was alone.

"Turn about with your backs to me, please, and lie facedown spread-eagled upon the floor," he said softly, and the two had nothing else to do but comply with his wishes.

"Me brand new suit—on that oily floor, begad!" swore Muldoon, protestingly.

The pistol nudged forward, so Scorchy subsided, grumbling.

They got down on the floor, and Ching gingerly approached, the white-faced newsboy at his side.

He bent to search them for weapons.

They looked at one another disgustedly. To have been captured at all was bad enough, but—without firing a shot?

And now the gang had three hostages.

CHAPTER 14

From the Shadows

As soon as Prince Zarkon left Savage's headquarters and descended to the street level, where Ace Harrigan was waiting with the car, he learned of Joey Weston's phone call. He also learned that Scorchy Muldoon and Nick Naldini had gone to investigate the warehouse where the mystery van was parked.

The Man from Tomorrow was naturally interested in the substance of Joey the newsboy's call. And it was even more natural that he was somewhat disgruntled by the fact that Scorchy and Nick had gone off to check it out. Ace sympathized with him.

"If I know those two goons, they'll get into a fracas first thing," volunteered the young aviator. Zarkon silently agreed. Neither the Irishman nor the stage magician were known for their timidity, and next to feuding with each other, the two loved best to jump into the middle of a free-for-all with the forces of evil.

Ace drove to the other side of town while Zarkon watched the Mayor's news conference on the portable televisor installed in the car.

Reaching the block, they circled it and spotted the Omega car parked where Muldoon and Naldini had left it.

"Looks like I was right," chuckled Ace Harrigan. "And I'll bet you dollars to peanuts, that's the kid's bike."

Zarkon nodded. "Pull up on the next street and we shall investigate," he directed. Ace pulled the limousine into a vacant parking space and the two men got out.

Zarkon and Harrigan entered the mouth of an alley and found a fire escape, which they climbed to the roof of the building nearest the warehouse. It was not Zarkon's intention to attempt to repeat his earlier entry into the abandoned house at Farmwell and Mountainair, where he had gotten in from the upper storey in order to rescue Scorchy from the thugs. Instead, he removed from an inner pocket of his jacket a pair of powerful binoculars, with which he scrutinized the interior of the warehouse, or as much of its interior as could be seen through the grimy windows.

"The van is still there," he remarked to Ace Harrigan. "At least, I assume it's the same van. The windows are so dirty that I cannot ascertain its color, but it seems in all other respects to match the descriptions of the vehicle."

Ace nodded. "How do we get in?" he asked, practical-minded as always.

Zarkon considered: Occupying the pier that jutted out into the river, the warehouse was too distant from their rooftop eyrie to try an entry from above. And it seemed foolhardy to risk charging the entrance, since they had no way of knowing how many crooks might be within the building, or how heavily they might be armed. "I'll try getting in the front," said Zarkon, "while you circle around the back and see if you can find an open window."

They descended the iron rungs of the fire-escape ladder and returned to the car, where Ace removed a suitcase from the trunk. In the back seat, both men donned one of Omega's special "business suits"—seemingly innocuous jackets and trousers whose linings were specially reinforced with light-weight metallic fiber and foam-plastic padding in order to render them virtually bulletproof.

They separated, Ace going around the back of the pier, searching for an open window like the one by which little Joey Weston had made his entry, while Zarkon approached from the front.

The door was locked from within, but Zarkon unlimbered a small device like a pocket-flashlight. The compact instrument projected a dazzling beam of coherent light wherewith he cut through the lock as easily as a laser beam would have.

Both men disappeared inside the building.

Yet another person was intrigued by the newsboy's phone call. This individual was Miss Phoenicia Mulligan. The blond heiress had only enjoyed a tantalizing morsel of excitement since this caper began, when she had been driving with Scorchy Muldoon at the time the crooks had rammed their car into the ditch in order to carry off the little prizefighter. And, frankly, she itched for a bit more fun.

The girl had yearned to accompany Muldoon and Naldini on their quest, but knew better than to speak up, knowing they would not permit her to venture into danger. Privately, Fooey Mulligan deplored this chivalrous, protective attitude, which implied that young women such as herself were unable to take care of themselves—which (in her case, at least) was certainly untrue.

So she waited around until after the two had departed, then quietly left headquarters muttering something about having a breakfast date with one of her old school chums. She hailed a cab and went to where Joey Weston had said the van had entered a warehouse.

Phoenicia Mulligan was not as well equipped for trouble as were the Omega men, with their "business suits" and pocket rayguns. But the adventure-loving girl had stowed away a small, wicked, ivory-handled revolver in her purse and regularly carried a bowie knife strapped to one pantyhose-clad inner thigh. She also had a practical working knowledge of judo and karate, and figured she was more than capable of taking on a couple of thugs, if it came to that.

And she rather hoped it *would* come to that.

By this time, the morning rush hour was well in progress, and her cab took its time weaving through the early traffic. Fortunately, the riverfront area where the warehouse was situated was slumping into decay, and few businesses thrived in that section of Knickerbocker City, so as soon as they came to the streets which ran beside the river, traffic died to a sluggish trickle and the cab made better time. But, all the while, Fooey was chafing impatiently in the rear seat.

82   *The Earth-Shaker*

"Hurry up, darn it," the girl muttered under her breath, "or all the fun will be over by the time I get there!"

The cab pulled up at the curb about a block and a half from the warehouse. Phoenicia Mulligan shoved a ten dollar bill into the hack driver's hand and didn't bother waiting for her change. She jumped out and slammed the door behind her.

"Nutty broad!" said the cab driver to himself, affectionately. "Tips me eight bucks for a two-buck fare . . . and where the heck is a good-looker like her goin' in this crummy neighborhood, I wonder?"

But he didn't stay around to find out.

Fooey scouted out the warehouse and found the front window which had been boarded up before Scorchy Muldoon kicked it in. The girl looked dubiously at the broken window, with its jagged shards of glass and splintered boarding, then glanced ruefully down at her expensive new dress, a flimsy morning frock purchased from a classy Park Avenue boutique.

"Well, what the hell!" the girl breathed, and determinedly clambered over the low sill.

"Oh, fooey!" she exclaimed, as a sharp splinter caught and ruined her hose. But she gamely continued on her way in the dingy building.

And immediately found herself facing a dramatic confrontation.

Ching faced the two Omega men, his gun leveled unwaveringly at their faces. The Oriental knew better than to aim the pistol at the torso or abdomen of the two, well aware from past experience how often Zarkon's lieutenants wore bulletproof suits.

"I said get down on the floor on your faces," he hissed at the duo. Scorchy glanced at Nick. Both had a number of small gadgets secreted away in their apparel which would help them out of tight situations like this, but they were afraid that, if they were to unlimber any of these, Ching might panic, start shooting wildly, and perhaps hit the boy, who stood white-faced at his side.

Scorchy, in particular, yearned to try one of his tricks. The heels of his shoes were loaded with flash-powder gimmicked to ignite in an eye-dazzling flare if he clicked his feet together in a certain fashion. Scorchy had employed this trick on more than one occasion, and it was one of his favorite devices. Indeed, he was so fond of it that he kept overloading the hollow heel to such an extent that Nick often joked Scorchy could blow off a foot if he wasn't careful.

But Ching was watching him alertly, ready for the slightest sign of just such a ploy.

"Oh, dang it all," groaned the pint-sized prizefighter, "my new suit, too!" But he got down on the floor beside Naldini, who was similarly annoyed. Nick was wearing a fancy, three-piece suit of dark blue cloth, with gray spats, watch chain and fob, and his get-up was also not the sort of suit he wished to ruin by spread-eagling himself on the oil-stained floor. But the expression on Ching's alert, cold-eyed face was dangerous, and the little, soft-spoken Chinese was a cunning and deadly adversary who was certainly not one to shrink from killing a foe in cold blood.

Ching had immobilized the two Omega men cleverly. With their faces to the floor, they could not easily tell his position, and with their arms spread out he presumed it was safe for him to fish through their pockets and disarm them of any weapons they might be carrying. Actually, he had no intention of wasting time trying to search his captives: He planned to knock both men unconscious, then wait for the knockout gas to wear off and his men to rouse themselves from their slumbers, before doing anything else.

Ching made one mistake. And it was to prove a costly one.

All of his concentration was fixed on the two Omega men, and he forgot about the little boy at his side. But the plucky lad had been waiting for just such an opportunity to present itself.

And kicked the Oriental in the leg!

Joey was wearing his sneakers, and the footwear was flexible and didn't pack much of a punch. But the boy was smart enough to have already thought of this, so when he lashed out with one foot he aimed it so that he kicked Ching in the back of the knee.

With a startled squawk, the little man went sprawling and Joey jumped on the hand that still clenched the gun and tried to wrest it from Ching's grip. The lithe Chinaman flung the boy from him and swerved the gun into firing position.

But he was too late.

"Hold it right there, you slant-eyed sonovagun!" yelled Fooey Mulligan from the shadows.

CHAPTER 15

Joey Thinks Quick

When the little newsboy kicked Ching, Scorchy Muldoon was able to catch sight of the act, because his head was turned to one side and he could see the Oriental out of the corner of his eye. The Irishman scrambled to his feet, as did Nick Naldini.

"Fooey, your arrival was in the proverbial nick of time!" drawled Nick, looking down annoyedly at his soiled clothing. He ambled over to remove Ching's pistol and to frisk the little man for any concealed weapons.

Scorchy beamed a cheerful grin in Phoenicia's direction, but reserved his attention for the boy, who stood grinning. The redhead slung one arm around the lad's shoulders and gave him a comradely hug.

"That wuz quick thinkin', kid," he said warmly. "You ain't hurt or nothin', are ya?"

Joey Weston shook his head. "Nossir," he said gamely. "The lug never laid a finger on me."

By this time, the workmen were beginning to recover from the effects of the gas gun and were sitting up and staring about them in bewildered fashion, shaking their groggy heads and trying to clear their wits. Scorchy and Nick wasted no time in checking them out for weapons. Then they began tying them up with a coil of rope found in one of the packing cases.

Scorchy tossed the handcuffs he generally carried in the inner pockets of his coat, and the newsboy caught them neatly.

"You git the honor of puttin' the cuffs on Ching," grinned the

Irishman, and the boy delightedly snapped the cuffs on the Asian, who regarded him inscrutably, his expression bland and noncommittal. But there was cold murder in his slitted eyes.

"Looks like you boys been going down manholes!" quipped the blond heiress with a glance at their garments, which had absorbed considerable grime and oil from the dirty floor.

Nick gave her a frosty glance which didn't quite come off. "If you had arrived on the scene two minutes earlier . . . ," he began, but gave it up with a rueful shrug. Actually, her appearance had been timely, and he knew it.

"So this is the famous van!" remarked Fooey, looking it over. "Guess they were busy repainting it when you mugs jumped them."

"That's why I hadda get in here, Mr. Muldoon," declared Joey Weston guiltily, "even though I promised you I'd stay outa trouble. I peeked in one of the windows and saw them disguising it—"

"Aw, don't worry about it," said Scorchy. "Ivverthin' worked out fer th' best—"

"Yeah, and my sawed-off colleague here is famous for rushing into trouble himself," remarked Naldini.

Zarkon's arrival on the scene at that moment probably nipped in the bud the loud quarrel which would inevitably have resulted from the vaudevillian's quip. The Nemesis of Evil took in the scene with a rapid but all-encompassing glance.

"Good work," he said quietly. Words of praise came seldom from his lips, and were rarely fulsome. But both men, and the young woman, swelled visibly. As for Joey, he was staring at the Man of Mystery with hero worship in his shining eyes.

"Gollywhoppers!" breathed the boy to himself. Spying him, Zarkon smiled and came over to the lad.

"We appreciate your assistance in this affair, young man," he said. "Your courage and quick thinking have performed a fine service to your fellow citizens and to Knickerbocker City itself."

Joey said nothing, but the expression on his face was more eloquent than words.

Zarkon turned to Ching. "You will spare yourself much difficulty if you cooperate," he said.

Ching hissed some phrase in an oriental language unfamiliar to any of his auditors, save for Zarkon himself.

Just then, Ace Harrigan appeared from the rear of the big room. He surveyed the scene disgustedly.

"Why do I always come in just a little too late to have any of the fun?" he inquired aggrievedly. "Anyway, Chief, there's a steel door in the back. Looks like a bank vault."

"Very well," said Zarkon. "Scorchy, Nick—check out the rest of the building. There may be others. Phoenicia, would you be so kind as to go outside and call the police? There is a phone booth on the corner, the one this young fellow used to call headquarters. Ask them to bring a vehicle large enough to accommodate our captives."

The girl was reluctant to leave the scene, because that steel door in the back sounded promising, but she was so smitten with Zarkon that all resistance ebbed whenever he addressed her—which was as seldom as he could without seeming impolite.

"What about me, Chief?" demanded Ace Harrigan.

"You will stay here and keep an eye on these men, and especially on our Asian friend," advised Zarkon. Then he turned away to investigate the steel door which the aviator had discovered.

He did not get very far.

As soon as the Mayor had finished with his news conference, he wasted no time in contacting Omega headquarters. Doc Jenkins was holding down the fort, along with Menlo Parker, and the big man took the call.

"I need to know what Prince Zarkon is planning to do about the threat against the Berkeley National Bank and Trust Company," said Phineas T. Bulver. Doc cleared his throat apologetically.

"Well, Yer Honor," the huge man said in his slow, careful way, "the Chief ain't—isn't—here right now, and I ain't—haven't—had a chance t' speak with him since—"

"Forget the grammar, dagnabit!" the Mayor growled, mopping perspiration from his bald brow. "D'you know what time it is?"

With his computer-like memory, Doc Jenkins seldom needed to

consult watches or clocks. "Twenty-seven minutes after eleven," he said automatically.

"Yep! And twelve noon is creepin' up pretty fast," snapped the Mayor. "Now, lissen here: I been cooperating with you boys, haven't I? I let yer boss keep the cops from cordoning off the State Fidelity Trust's block, and look what happened! In a half an hour, a little more, I'm afraid the same thing's gonna happen to the Berkeley. Can you say I'm wrong?"

"Well . . ." admitted Doc Jenkins.

"Well—nothing! Either you Omega fellas got a plan or you ain't," snarled the Mayor, proving that he could be as ungrammatical as Doc Jenkins when his temper was frayed.

"Tell him we're coverin' it," whispered Menlo Parker in Doc Jenkins' ear. The skinny little scientist had come into the room just in time to catch the last part of the conversation. Doc gave him a goggle-eyed glance of mute inquiry, to which Menlo only replied with an emphatic gesture.

"We're, um, we're coverin' it, Yer Honor. Don't worry," said Doc into the phone.

"You better be," the Mayor declared in ominous tones before hanging up.

Replacing the phone on its hook, he sat back in his swivel chair and gloomily looked around the room that was his office. There frowned down at him a dozen or more oil portraits of former mayors of Knickerbocker City, from the one-legged Dutchman who had first occupied that position, way back before the Revolutionary War, to his most recent predecessor, now a senator in Washington.

"Well, what are you ginks glarin' at?" demanded the Mayor irritably. "None o' you guys ever hadda face a spook like this Earth-Shaker back in yer day!"

None of the portraits deigned to reply.

Doc hung up the phone and turned on the skinny scientist.

"Whaddaya mean 'tell him we're coverin' it'?" he demanded accusingly.

"Because we will be," Menlo snapped. "You big oaf, don't you re-

alize everybody has had fun with this caper except us? Even that—
female—has had some excitement. So—"

"So?" repeated Doc, beginning to grin as he caught the drift of
Menlo's words.

"So it's up to us to get to the Berkeley bank and check things
out," said Parker suavely. "We can call the Chief and the boys on
the way."

"We're s'posed to stick around and watch the phones," Jenkins
reminded him. Menlo flapped his hands irritably.

"Chandra Lal can do *that!*" he said scathingly. "C'mon—you
gonna let me go alone, and have all the fun?"

"I'm with ya," said the big man happily.

They took one of the cars and drove off in a hurry.

CHAPTER 16

Return from the Dead

As Zarkon approached the steel door in the rear of the warehouse, working his way carefully through boxes and bales, a ground-glass screen lit up unexpectedly. It was set into the brick wall above the door, and now it glowed with light and swirling hues, which gradually resolved themselves into a clear picture.

It was the visage of a bald, bullet-headed man whose grim, heavy-jawed face was swathed in white bandages like the wrappings of a mummy. Seemingly opaque black goggles covered his eyes, and little of his flesh was visible between the bandages.

Early in his career, however, Prince Zarkon had made an extensive study of the science of physiognomy, and did not have to see a man's face unmasked in order to recognize him, for the bone structure of the face and skull alone are as distinctive, almost, as fingerprints.

As he recognized the man in the televisor screen, the Man from Tomorrow experienced a distinct shock of disbelief. For the man who glowered down at him from the ground-glass panel he knew to be dead.

It would seem that the other recognized him as well, despite the dim light, the deep shadows, and the black goggles he wore over his eyes.

"So we meet again, Prince Zarkon!" he purred gloatingly, his voice issuing from a small microphone set beneath the televisor screen.

"So it would seem, Lucifer," replied Zarkon quietly. His features were as inscrutable as those of his adversary masked in bandages. They did not reveal the consternation, the shock, the alarm that seethed in his breast. For the man in the screen was an old and deadly adversary—perhaps the most dangerous criminal alive on earth.

Dr. Zandor Sinestro smiled grimly. The brilliant but deranged scientist had long since declared war against society, deliberately choosing one of the names of the Devil by which to be known by men.

"Doubtless, you believed me dead in the conflagration which destroyed my mountain laboratory," said Lucifer. "And indeed, as you can see, I suffered extensive, if superficial, burn damage, which I am still recovering from. Soon the skin and tissue grafts will be completed, and I will be able to show my face before the world once more."

Zarkon said nothing. It seemed all but impossible to him that the fire had not indeed slain Lucifer, but he knew the super-criminal to be a cunning and wily and resourceful scientist, and trusted him to have a few tricks up his sleeve.*

Zarkon, of course, had a few tricks of his own. As he began to engage the Earth-Shaker in quiet conversation, he unobtrusively pressed one elbow against his side. Secreted in the lining of his jacket was a small alarm signal attuned to similar instruments lodged in the belt buckles worn by his men.

Zarkon pressed the signal thrice. In Omega code, "three" was the signal to get out in a hurry.

Zarkon did not put it past his arch-enemy to have wired the entire warehouse to explode. He was willing to risk his own life in the struggle against Lucifer, but not the lives of his lieutenants, for whom he felt a deep, warm friendship and admiration that would have surprised them had they known it, since Zarkon generally presented a detached and coldly emotionless face even to those closest to him.

"Your attempts to extort millions from the banking community of

---

* The previous encounter between Zarkon and Lucifer, alluded to above, is recounted in the first volume of these memoirs, a book entitled *The Nemesis of Evil*, published by Doubleday in 1975.

Knickerbocker City were foredoomed to failure," Zarkon said, playing for time and spinning out the conversation to give his friends a chance to get out of the building before Lucifer used his trump card. "It is a pity, Lucifer, that you turned to crime. Your genius is such that it would have earned you the supreme accolades of the scientific world, had you chosen to serve civilization, rather than striving to undermine and destroy it."

Lucifer sneered. "This scientific community of which you speak consists of a bewildered pack of shortsighted dolts," he said. "I desire neither their praise nor their honors. And as for this civilization you preach of, it is a herd of ignorant, superstitious cattle, hungry for a man of power to assume the supreme command over their lives."

"Then, your goal is to create a dictatorship, with yourself, of course, in the highest position of authority?" queried Zarkon.

The other laughed sardonically. "Say, rather, as God-Emperor!" he proclaimed. And then, in his mercurial way, Lucifer changed his tones. "I would that you would join me in my cause, Prince Zarkon," he said softly. "Together, we could turn this world into a veritable utopia, devoid of crime, poverty, sickness and war. Your own scientific genius coupled to mine—"

"You know that can never be," said Zarkon gently. "I came here to serve and protect mankind, not to dominate it."

"Yes, I know . . . it is a pity! With you at my side—at my right hand!—we could transform the world within a generation, even a decade. Alas, that I must shoulder the task alone, but so be it. And —*farewell!*"

From a small, round opening just beneath the microphone, a blinding beam of laser-bright death stabbed directly at the tall figure of the Master of Mysteries. . . .

Menlo and Doc Jenkins pulled up across the street from the Berkeley National Bank and Trust Company, and parked beneath a shady tree.

"Sure hope you got an ace up yer sleeve, Menlo," groused Doc Jenkins tiredly. The big man rubbed his red-rimmed eyes and gave a jaw-cracking yawn. None of the Omega men had gotten any sleep the night before, although Phoenicia Mulligan had snatched a cat-nap on the sofa, and the strain of worry and fatigue was beginning to show.

"Stop gripin', dang it!" snapped Menlo Parker irritably. He was as weary as his huge comrade, and his temper, usually pretty short, was frayed raw.

"Yeah, but you heard the Mayor," said Doc Jenkins. "If we flub this one, it's the last time he'll keep the cops from cordoning off the street and emptyin' the nearby buildings. . . ."

"Mayor Bulver's a nervous old maid," commented Menlo Parker. "The bank's empty, 'cause he got the Governor to declare today a bank holiday, so nobody's gonna get hurt. And them other buildings aren't in danger, 'cause you know the Earth-Shaker always strikes directly on target, shakin' down one building and only one building. So—what's there to be scared of?"

"Hope yer right," yawned the big man.

Menlo was engaged in setting up a variety of sensitive instruments.

Doc Jenkins watched him with dull eyes for a moment, then spoke up again. "How d'yuh suppose this Earth-Shaker guy does it, Menlo?" he inquired. "Explosives buried unnerground, or something? There's a lotta tunnels and subway tracks and sewers an' stuff under the streets. Easy enough to plant bombs. . . ."

"Danged if I know," said the little scientist savagely. "But I stayed up all night goin' over them seismograph readings we got when the Earth-Shaker brought down the State Fidelity Trust. Th' Chief and I agree: a natural earthquake, plain as the nose on yer face. Explosives woulda left a whole different set of tracks."

Jenkins rubbed the offending member thoughtfully, with another huge yawn. "Whaddaya think, Menlo? Is Lucifer this Earth-Shaker guy? Dunno how he *could* be, since he died in that fire inside Mount Shasta, but . . . Ching's mixed up in this. And Ching usta be his right-hand man."

"Wouldn't trust Lucifer not to have more lives than the proverbial cat," muttered Menlo abstractedly, fiddling with dial settings.

"Mebbe Ching's set himself up in business on his own—now hush up, Doc, this is tricky business here!"

Jenkins subsided. He looked out the car window. The street was deserted, cordon or no cordon, and if anybody was still in the fancy apartment buildings which lined both sides of the street, nobody was showing his face.

The sun was high up in a pale blue sky. Everything was deathly still. It was as if all of Nature was holding its breath, waiting for the sinister Earth-Shaker to strike for the third time.

"Now, that's funny," murmured Menlo Parker.

"What is?" inquired Doc sleepily.

Menlo cocked a thumb at the dashboard of the car.

"Look at the clock, dummy!" Jenkins did so, then voiced a grunt of surprise.

"Hey . . . it's five minutes past noon!" he exclaimed.

Menlo Parker nodded slowly. He looked around at the silent, untenanted street. Nothing had happened . . . absolutely nothing at all!

"I don't git this, Menlo," complained Doc Jenkins bewilderedly. The big man looked injured, an expression he always assumed when confronted by something his brilliantly accurate, computer-like mind could not understand.

"Me neither," muttered Menlo Parker ungrammatically.

The two men exchanged a mystified glance.

The hands of the clock crept on. It got to be ten after twelve, then a quarter past.

They felt amazement. For this was the first time the mysterious Earth-Shaker had ever failed to strike exactly at the announced time. . . .

But . . . *why?*

CHAPTER 17

Menlo Parker, Hero

When their belt-buckle receivers picked up Prince Zarkon's alarm signal, the Omega men wasted no time in bundling out of the warehouse. Scorchy grumbled at missing whatever fun was about to commence, and Nick Naldini snarled a string of Italian curses, but the crime-fighters knew better than to disobey a direct order in Omega code. And besides, there were Phoenicia Mulligan and little Joey Weston to worry about.

They crossed the street and took refuge behind the Omega car, because it had already occurred to them, as to Zarkon, that the Earth-Shaker might well have planted dynamite to blow up his headquarters, rather than be taken alive. While they were crouched behind the vehicle, Ace helped the newsboy put the borrowed bike in the trunk of the car for safety.

People were long since up and around, and cars zipped past while men in dirty overalls and shabby work clothes slouched along the sidewalks and intersections. If the warehouse blew up now, the Omega men muttered worriedly, a lot of innocent people could be hurt or even killed. . . .

But nothing happened. Except that the police arrived in droves, answering the call from the corner booth, and so did enough paddywagons to haul off the captives.

"We left them poor guys behind, all tied up," exclaimed Ace Harrigan. "Ching, too!" And they looked at one another a trifle nervously. As far as they were concerned, privately, each of the Omega men figured that a cold-blooded crook like Ching deserved nothing better than to be blown up along with the building, if it came to that. But Zarkon had severe rules against the unnecessary loss of life, and they knew how disappointed he would be in his men if he found out that they had wantonly risked the lives of eight men, criminals or not.

Scorchy Muldoon sneaked a look across the hood of the car. The building stood unchanged as before, seemingly empty and abandoned. If it was going to explode, what was taking it so long?

"Here comes the lieutenant," muttered Nick Naldini. He got to his feet and ambled out to discuss the situation with the police officer.

"I'll call the Bomb Squad. And order up some ambulances," the cop said, heading at a sprint for his patrol car and its radio.

"Better git the Fire Department, too!" yelled the little prizefighter after him.

Fooey Mulligan was getting restive. She was beginning to fume a little. "Are you goons just going to squat here on your heels, when Zarkon's in danger?" she demanded hotly. They gave her shamefaced looks and sheepish grins. Not one man among them but would have happily risked his life to protect his leader . . . but orders were orders.

"Well, fooey on the lot of you!" the blond girl sniffed. And she trotted across the street and vanished into the warehouse before any of them, or the police officers, could stop her.

"Okay, I'm goin' in too," declared Scorchy Muldoon. "If'n only to drag Fooey out by her heels!"

Nick gave a nasty, sniggering laugh. "It'd take two dwarfs the size of you to carry out a big gal like Fooey Mulligan," he drawled wickedly.

Scorchy flushed until his cheeks burned the same hot shade as his tousled hair. "Why, you vaudeville clown—" he started to huff, then shrugged. "C'mon!"

They crossed the street and entered the building again, followed by the police.

The sizzling bolt of electric fire knocked Zarkon over backwards. He sprawled limply, a dark form against the shadowed floor. From the televisor screen, Lucifer surveyed the limp figure narrowly. Smoke trickled from singed cloth. The sprawled form did not move.

"So passes a worthy adversary," sighed Lucifer, "and a great champion of civilization! What a pity to destroy such a brilliant intellect. . . ."

Despite the mock sorrow in his voice, a lurking undertone of gloating satisfaction gave a clue as to his real feelings.

The televisor went dark.

Zarkon rose to his feet and concealed himself behind a crate. There, with a pocket-flashlight, he examined his clothing ruefully.

"A good thing I wore a 'business suit,'" said the Champion of Justice to himself.

And indeed it was! The metallic fibers in the protective lining had harmlessly conducted the electric bolt into the floor, merely singeing the cloth a trifle.

Had the bolt come from a laser, however, Zarkon would have been dead that very moment, or dangerously wounded. But he was unharmed, merely shaken a little.

On swift, light feet he ran toward the front of the building, still half expecting it to be destroyed in an explosion any moment. There he found Phoenicia Mulligan cussing a blue streak as Nick and Scorchy forcibly ejected her onto the street. Cops were swarming over the place, lugging out the workmen who had been gassed while disguising the van. Zarkon surveyed the scene grimly.

One captive was missing.

Of course, it was Ching. The wily Chinaman was not easily held, even by steel handcuffs. Where he had gotten to, nobody could guess.

The police drove the van out onto the street, and forensic experts began examining it for prints and other clues. They discovered no apparatus within the vehicle which could account for the mysterious earthquake disasters.

Scorchy came up to where Zarkon stood.

"Chief, the Mayor's on th' line, yelling like a banshee," said the prizefighter. "Seems the Earth-Shaker wuz s'posed to wreck another bank at noon, but—"

Zarkon glanced quickly at his watch. The dial read twenty minutes after twelve.

"—but he didn't!" finished Scorchy with a huge grin.

"I'm not surprised," admitted Zarkon thoughtfully. "It would seem that the van was somehow instrumental in causing the quakes. Without it, the quakes will not occur. Odd."

The members of the Bomb Squad had arrived on the scene by this time and were filing in, looking like weird monsters from another world in their armored protective suits. Zarkon and the others quitted the building so the experts could get to work.

Menlo and Doc Jenkins exchanged faintly incredulous glances as the hands of the dashboard clock crept on, and on, and on. A moment later, the dashboard light began blinking, and Doc picked up the radiophone. He listened for a moment, then replaced the instrument and turned to his wizened companion with a huge, foolish grin.

"Hizzoner is on the way," the man with the computer brain announced. "So's the police commissioner. Seems they both wanna congratulate ya, Menlo!"

"But I didn't *do* anything!" said the waspish savant plaintively.

"Yeah, but *they* don't know that!" chuckled Doc. "Mayor's whoopin' and hollerin' about how he'll never doubt Omega again."

Menlo Parker looked dubious.

A few minutes later, cars arrived in droves, and cops, city officials and reporters began piling out.

The Honorable Phineas T. Bulver came waddling over to where the two Omega operatives stood waiting for him. Beaming with jovial good humor and chortling with relief, mopping his damp red brow with a bandanna handkerchief of much the same hue, the Mayor of Knickerbocker City shook their hands.

"Dagnabit, but you young fellers did the trick this time!" he crowed. "Dunno how you did it—trade secret, I betcha!—but that dagnab Earth-Shaker's cowering in his hidey-hole this minute, licking his wounds!"

Menlo gulped embarrassedly, stammering for awkward words.

The Mayor wrung his bony hand in a crushing grip, and Menlo gave a weak smile. Flashbulbs were popping on all sides.

"That was good work, Dr. Parker, Mr. Jenkins," the police commissioner chimed in. He was a tall, lean, distinguished-looking man in his early fifties, and formed a striking contrast to the fat little Mayor at his side.

But Doc and Menlo knew him to be one of the smartest and toughest cops ever to rise to prominence through the ranks of the city's detective squads, and a man of few words and fewer compliments.

"Yessir, boys," puffed the Mayor, turning to face the mob of reporters, "you can quote me as sayin' that that dagnab Zarkon has chased the Earth-Shaker inta hidin' and we'll be havin' an arrest in no time flat!"

"Oh, my," groaned Menlo feebly. Then he tried to muster a proud, confident smile for the cameramen.

"Let's get the heck outa here," mumbled Doc Jenkins in his partner's ear.

Menlo nodded vigorously. "Yeah, let's get back to headquarters, where it's nice an' quiet," he said feelingly.

They drove back to the block of fake building-fronts, and felt happy once the door was shut behind them.

"Chandra, rustle up some grub fer a coupla hungry heroes, will ya?" asked Doc. "After all, we just saved the whole blame' city from destruction, t' hear Mayor Bulver tell it!"

The tall Rajput smiled briefly and bowed and vanished into his kitchen. Seconds later, delicious odors seeped through the half-closed door and they heard the sound of bubbling pots.

Doc collapsed into the sofa. "Why'n'cha get on the horn, Menlo, and see where the boys are? Even Fooey Mulligan seems to have taken off."

Menlo did, reappearing moments later with relief visible on his face. For Zarkon had explained why the third bank had not been destroyed like the first two. And Menlo was never happier than when a problem was solved.

CHAPTER 18

The Earth-Shaker Vanishes

As soon as the policemen of the Bomb Squad had ascertained that the building was not mined with explosives, Zarkon and his men returned to the warehouse.

The steel door in the rear was soon cut through by means of oxyacetylene torches. They found the elevator and the steel lockers which Ching had earlier used. These had been rigged with thermite charges which could be electrically ignited from an inner room, and their contents were destroyed. They found the remains of the instrument box which the Oriental had carried from the van, but could deduce little therefrom. It was a mere lump of fused metal and charred plastic by now.

The big, bank-vault door would have taken hours to open with the torches, so Zarkon opened it himself. He used the same superstethoscope device he had employed in searching the house on the corner of Mountainair and Farmwell streets. Making minute adjustments to the dial and listening intently to the click of the tumblers, he picked the complex lock in less than forty seconds.

Nick Naldini swore admiringly. The stage magician was a clever man, with nimble fingers, and had formerly made a living of sorts as a cardsharp, pickpocket and in even less reputable trades. He had opened a safe or two in the old days, had Nick, and he knew the proportions of Zarkon's feat.

They entered the white-tiled room where Lucifer had sat in the wheelchair under the dazzle of lights, but found it, of course, empty.

Zarkon had expected nothing less. Even though Lucifer believed him slain by the electric ray, the master criminal would not have lingered about these premises any longer than it took to ignite the thermite in the files and steel lockers, destroying whatever evidence might have been stashed within, before making his getaway.

What was of premier interest to Zarkon right now was to find out exactly how the Earth-Shaker had, in fact, made that getaway. He had a hunch, concerning which he had given no hint to his men, but he was still putting together bits and pieces of information.

The laboratory had been outfitted like a surgical clinic. Obviously, herein had Lucifer been given the skin grafts which were restoring his burned body to normalcy. Probably, the grafts had been given him by physicians attached to the underworld, who were retained by gang-leaders for such illicit medical work as bullet wounds and the like.

They searched the lab room quickly but thoroughly but found nothing of any particular interest.

Behind the laboratory they found storerooms and a well-equipped workshop filled with delicate apparatus. Behind these was an elegantly furnished apartment and a small but compact kitchen. The apartment was decorated with taste and displayed a wide range of cultured interests indicative of Lucifer's complex and contradictory personality.

Scorchy looked around at the sumptuous hangings and select oil paintings, the china and crystal, and his lips formed a silent whistle.

"Does himself okay, the crook," muttered the Irishman. Nick was marveling at the oriental rugs, which were virtually priceless.

"Yeah . . . who says crime doesn't pay?" he cracked sardonically.

Zarkon said nothing, being occupied with rapidly skimming the bookshelves. They were loaded with scientific texts and references in several languages but told him little.

"Look here, Chief," Ace Harrigan said, calling his attention to file folders on a low table.

Zarkon examined them briefly.

"What d'you suppose Lucifer wanted with these marine charts?"

asked the handsome aviator. "Geological survey maps of the area I can understand, but why these?"

Zarkon said nothing.

Before long, they found an elevator concealed behind a sliding panel and took it to a subbasement somehow built below the pier on which the warehouse stood. It seemed likely that this was the means by which Lucifer had escaped from the building, knowing that it would soon be swarming with cops.

The room was square and simple. There were compressors and air pumps, but nothing else.

Nothing except a circular opening in the floor, through which they could see the surface of the river and hear waves sloshing and gurgling around the pilings which supported the structure.

Phoenicia Mulligan stared uncomprehendingly at the well-like aperture.

"What the heck is *that* for?" the blond heiress murmured to no one in particular.

"Danged if *I* know," admitted Scorchy Muldoon.

Zarkon was examining a series of tubes and lines which descended from an overhead frame, disappearing into the dark waters beneath the pier. It seemed to be a suspension system of some kind, but one the likes of which neither Scorchy nor the others had ever seen before.

"What is it, Chief?" asked Nick Naldini.

Zarkon rarely gave explanations until he was in possession of all the facts, but he did so now. It was not that the Lord of the Unknown was particularly secretive by nature, but simply that he did not like to speak until he was certain of all details. "A bathysphere," he remarked. "Obviously, the means by which Lucifer escaped."

"A *whatz*isphere?" asked little Joey Weston.

Zarkon smiled. "A diving bell," he said succinctly. Even the newsboy had heard of diving bells, which were sometimes used for underwater explorations. Scorchy and the others stared at one another incredulously.

"Begorra, are you tryin' to tell us that Lucifer's sittin' on the bottom of the river in a divin' bell, Chief?" the Irishman asked. "Then, we got him trapped! All the cops gotta do is get a strong winch down here and haul the bell back up to the surface. . . ."

Zarkon shook his head meditatively. "I doubt if he is still within the device," he replied.

"Yeah, that wouldn't make much sense, would it?" Phoenicia said. "If he's got enough brains to make phony earthquakes, he's plenty smart enough not to get himself trapped on the bottom of the river."

"Well, whadda we do now?" inquired Scorchy Muldoon.

Zarkon said nothing. They seemed to have reached a dead end. Whatever mode of transport the Earth-Shaker had employed after his descent in the bathysphere, he was doubtless far away by this time. They had run out of leads, and their search of the warehouse had turned up no clues worth thinking about. Unless the police lab experts came up with something, the case had reached an impasse.

"So where do we go from here, Chief?" asked Ace Harrigan.

"Back to headquarters," Zarkon said briefly, "for some much-needed sleep."

Back at headquarters, they ate the meal which their Hindu servant had prepared, and traded stories with Menlo and Doc Jenkins.

"Sure wish Lucifer hadn't fired those lockers," muttered the skinny little scientist yearningly. "Did there seem to be lots of papers in 'em, Chief?"

Zarkon indicated that such was the case.

"Forensics has gathered up the charred remains and will be trying to piece them together so that they can be read under infrared light," he added. "You understand the technique."

"Then, we may get some clue to what's been goin' on, after all," commented Menlo. Zarkon nodded.

"I'm gonna get some shut-eye," murmured Fooey Mulligan, "if it's okay with you fellows." The blond heiress had taken a suite in the Marlborough Hotel for her visit to Knickerbocker City, but Zarkon put one of the several apartments in his headquarters at her disposal. She was in this adventure up to her neck by now, and the

Master of Fate knew there was no keeping her out of things now, so he might as well take the path of least resistance.

"Joey can bunk in with me, Chief," declared Scorchy Muldoon, who had taken an instant liking to the little newsboy. They had planned to drive Joey back to his rooming house, but the lad had fallen asleep in the back of the car, so they took him back with them to headquarters.

"Better give his folks a call," said Fooey. "They must be pretty worried by now."

"Naw," grinned the pint-sized prizefighter. "Kid ain't got no folks; he's an orphan, like me. I got a extra cot in my digs. He won't take up much room."

Doc Jenkins, with a succession of jaw-cracking yawns, began setting up several gadgets. These would arouse the Omega men from their rest if a call came in from the Mayor, the commissioner, or the police laboratory that was trying to make something out of the burned papers, but would simply record any other calls, such as those from newspaper reporters.

"All set, Chief," the big man mumbled, rubbing his eyes sleepily.

They turned in for some much-needed sack time.

And awoke to learn that during their sleep the Earth-Shaker had interrupted the television broadcasts to threaten that he would next destroy the block of buildings which housed Omega headquarters!

CHAPTER 19

Omega in Peril

They gathered in the big front room to listen to the tape of Lucifer's message. The criminal mastermind had somehow interrupted the transmission of every local television station simultaneously, probably by overriding the carrier waves with a more powerful signal.

While the Omega men had been sleeping when the message flashed on television screens across the city and, indeed, across the nation, it had been taped by one of the local stations. The Amalgamated News Service, which had cooperated with Prince Zarkon several times in the past, had procured a copy of the complete message and had rushed the tape to Zarkon's headquarters.

They took their seats as Doc Jenkins fed the videotape into the apparatus.

The screen lit up with portions of an early-afternoon game show of remarkable mindlessness. The game-show host's vapid grin blurred, resolving into the grim visage of a hooded man who stared directly into the camera with malignant eyes. Despite the hood (obviously donned to conceal his scarred and bandaged visage), they at once recognized him as Lucifer, the Earth-Shaker.

His deep, slow, ominous tones rang out in the tense stillness of the big room:

"Citizens of Knickerbocker City, this is the Earth-Shaker speaking! Your municipal officials and banking institutions have thus far stubbornly refused to accept my ultimatums, and I have been forced to demolish two of your most distinguished banking institutions: the

Jefferson National Bank and Trust Company, and the State Fidelity Trust.

"I know full well that your police force is powerless to stop me, for my whereabouts remain unknown, although I have twice demonstrated my power to move the very earth beneath your feet. . . ."

Zarkon's men noticed that Lucifer made no reference to his failure to similarly wreck the Berkeley bank. Since neither Ching, the van nor the mysterious instrument box had been available, they understood why the Earth-Shaker's third crime had failed to come off. But how like the megalomaniacal Lucifer to grandly ignore the failure as if he had never made the third threat!

"The only opposition which has proved at all effective against my plans has been the Omega organization, led by the brilliant and courageous Prince Zarkon. Zarkon, I salute you! You are truly an adversary worthy of my steel, and I rejoice that you escaped death before my electric ray."

Zarkon's features displayed no emotion. Of course, the afternoon papers had been full of his exploits and those of his aides. It had not taken Lucifer very long to discover that he had not been destroyed by the bolt. But Zarkon had never seriously considered striving to delude his adversary on this point by pretending death, for such had seemed pointless to him.

The cunning criminal mastermind was not easily fooled anyway, and to have gone into hiding while directing the efforts of his lieutenants from behind the scenes would have crippled, or at least drastically hampered, his freedom of movement.

Lucifer continued: "For my next step, I have decided to revise my original plans: Instead of demolishing the financial institutions which fail to comply with my directives—and the names of these are already known to you, having been widely published—I have chosen to strike at Omega itself. And I challenge Zarkon and his operatives to stop me!"

The cold eyes bored directly into their own, it seemed, as deadly and remorseless as the eyes of a cobra. For all their bravery and intestinal fortitude, the Omega men could not help shivering a little before the icy menace in that implacable and unblinking gaze.

"Therefore, I herewith hurl the gauntlet at the very feet of the so-called Lord of the Unknown! Zarkon, you have my challenge: At one o'clock tomorrow morning, it is my intention to utterly destroy the entire block of buildings in which the headquarters of the Omega organization are situated.

"This will be the largest and most devastating earthquake which as yet I have caused, and should demonstrate once and for all time that I hold supreme power of life and death over the very metropolis of Knickerbocker City! Unless my demands are met, following the total destruction of Omega, I will, if necessary, level the entire city. That this will cause the loss of many thousands of lives is a matter of grave concern to me, naturally—"

"Cold-blooded hypocrite!" hissed Miss Phoenicia Mulligan from clenched teeth.

Zarkon gestured the blond girl to silence.

"—but that the resultant damage will be numbered in the thousands of millions of dollars is a matter of no concern whatsoever! For the greedy and unscrupulous hands which control the entire financial resources of Knickerbocker City are deaf to my most reasonable demands. Should they remain so, adamantly refusing to accept my ultimatum, the fall of this mighty metropolis is upon their guilty souls, not mine!

"One final word, if you will permit me! Zarkon, I am not heartless—your life means as much to me as it does to the helpless citizens you have given your career to protect and defend. Surrender to me and give yourself over into my hands; then the walls of Omega shall remain unshaken by . . . the Earth-Shaker. If not, farewell!"

Zarkon leaned forward, staring intently at the hooded face on the television screen.

"If you agree to surrender in good faith—and I, in turn, promise that you will not be harmed in any way—then come tonight to the Golden Apple Club, on Fourteenth Street, where you will be given a certain message. Come alone and unarmed, and be certain that you are there by the very stroke of midnight, or before the world has grown an hour older, Omega will cease to exist.

"For all your courage and intelligence, you are helpless to resist my power to move the very earth. Surrender, Zarkon—or die!"

And with those ringing words, the image faded and was briefly replaced by the features of the game-show host, before the videotape ended.

Zarkon continued staring at the screen, his virile features tense, absorbed in thought.

Phoenicia looked fearfully at him. She had a horrible suspicion that Zarkon would actually surrender to his arch-enemy, in order to spare the lives of his lieutenants and the continuance of the crime-fighting team he had welded together with his unique genius.

Her lips parted to ask if he really intended to do it—to argue that he knew there was no trusting the word of the sinister criminal mastermind, but Zarkon abruptly spoke before her lips had time to shape the words.

"Doc, what do you know about the Golden Apple?" he inquired tersely. The big man pursed his lips, rummaging through the infallible super-memory of his amazing mind.

"Well, Chief, not much, actually!" Jenkins said hesitantly. "Back in the early 1940s, it was a sort of fashionable gambling palace and nightclub, run by a gang of hoods. Manager was a gink called Chips O'Hearn . . . cops closed the place down coupla times . . . eventually it was bought up by some real estate combine or other, and it's been straight enough ever since—"

Zarkon cut him off with a curt gesture. Then, surprisingly, he turned to Fooey Mulligan.

"Phoenicia, would you do me a favor? It may involve some danger, but I believe not."

"Why, certainly—I'd be glad to help!" the blond heiress said in surprised tones.

"Thank you. Then, tonight, at ten o'clock, perhaps you will permit Ace to escort you to the nightclub? There are some things I would like the two of you to check out, before my own arrival."

"Hot dog!" grinned Ace. The aviator privately considered Fooey Mulligan a forty-carat stunner, which in fact she was. Nobody else had a chance to get a date with her, he knew, not so long as Zarkon was in the vicinity. But the crack pilot was delighted to get her alone with wine and candlelight and soft, romantic music.

"You ain't really goin' to this joint, are you, Chief?" demanded Scorchy Muldoon aggrievedly. "You know you can't trust that bum, Lucifer. He's tried to fry yer gizzard before, and he'd love nothin' more than fer you t' just walk into his trap!"

"Don't worry about me, Scorchy," advised the Ultimate Man.

The Omega men got busy, having rested sufficiently to recover from their long sequence of adventures. There were many small instruments to be assembled, several devices to be removed from the storage rooms, and plans to be made.

The telephones had been ringing all day, with every paper and TV newscaster and reporter in the city requesting an interview with Zarkon. His men ignored the calls, for any really important message would come over a special line which had nothing to do with the other phones. Only the Mayor, the police commissioner, and the Federal Bureau of Investigation had *that* phone number, so the other ringing phones could simply be ignored.

Afternoon shadows lengthened. Fooey went back to her hotel, and reappeared ready for her date with Ace Harrigan. He was faultlessly attired in black tie and dinner jacket rig, but she stole the whole show. For this occasion, she had dragged out of the mothballs a fabulous gown of platinum lamé, off the shoulder, with a deep neckline, and it fit like a glove, displaying to fullest advantage her rather breathtaking contours.

The two departed that evening, for dining and dancing.

Joey Weston, rather neglected, looked around puzzledly.

For Zarkon had vanished.

CHAPTER 20

The Golden Apple

The two departed for the nightclub in one of Omega's cars, a black Supra limousine. Fooey Mulligan was delighted, and Ace Harrigan looked supremely pleased with himself. The handsome aviator, like most of the Omega men (with the obvious exception of that devout misogynist, Menlo Parker) had been trying to get a date with the blond heiress since her arrival here in Knickerbocker City, but without success. She was so stuck on Prince Zarkon, whom she had met on a Pacific island under the most romantic of circumstances, that she couldn't see another man.

So it was no wonder that Ace was pleased. And, to be sure, in his faultless evening clothes, he looked tanned and terrific, the veritable answer to a maiden's prayer.

The maiden in question, however, was delighted not so much by being taken by the handsome young aviator to a fashionable nightclub for an evening of what was ostensibly to be fun, frivolity and feasting, but simply because Prince Zarkon had asked her to help him in this matter. Miss Phoenicia Mulligan had been long accustomed to having men fall all over themselves to win her favors, since about age fifteen, in fact. But Zarkon was the only bachelor, eligible or ineligible, who had for so long stubbornly and patiently resisted her onslaught of charms.

To do him this favor was to place him, albeit slightly, in her debt, the girl thought cunningly. Well, what's wrong with that? "All's fair in love and—whatever-it-was," she concluded smugly.

They pulled up in front of the Golden Apple, and Ace Harrigan, tossing the keys to a parking attendant, escorted her from the limousine into the sumptuous interior.

The nightclubs of Knickerbocker City had long since passed their heyday, when Whozis was wont to drink champagne from Whatzis' slipper. Still and all, the place, living anachronism or no, had decided to capitalize on the drawback, and deliberately cultivated old-time Jazz Age nostalgia in its ostentatious Art Deco ornamentation and in a menu written in three languages, with prices that would have made a Texas oilman gasp.

The two took their seats and sipped cocktails while a lavish orchestra played a rhumba, then a tango, then a cha-cha. After an appropriate interval, Ace excused himself and retired to the washroom, where, finding himself alone, he employed the several small and lightweight devices unobtrusively hidden away in his faultlessly tailored tux.

He returned, looking faintly baffled.

They sipped another cocktail. Then Phoenicia excused herself and retired to the powder room, where she ran a series of similar tests. Exasperated by her failure to turn up anything of concrete interest, she pretended to blunder into the kitchen, was politely redirected, blundered into various mop closets and such, and eventually wandered back to the table to rejoin her escort.

Masking their *sotto voce* conference behind bright, flirtatious smiles, they exchanged notes.

"I can't find anything wrong with this place," confessed Ace Harrigan. "Checked the back walls and side walls with the sonic detector, but no hidden rooms . . . used the electronic detector, but no suspicious wiring or anything. . . ."

"Same here," admitted Fooey Mulligan. The blond girl had employed similar instruments on the other side of the rear, where the powder room was situated. "Where d'you suppose they had the gambling part hidden away? I couldn't detect any hidden rooms on my side."

Ace shrugged. "Doc Jenkins says after the last big raid, the cops closed the joint down. It was sold to new owners, and they walled up the gambling part. It's now been torn down and made into a parking lot for patrons."

"Let's keep at it. We aren't here for our health, you know," suggested the girl. Ace looked aggrieved.

"How about a turn on the dance floor?" he asked. "I do a real mean tango—"

"Business, not pleasure," snapped the heiress from behind a coy smile. Harrigan shrugged unhappily, but complied.

The evening wore on. They downed a light snack of hors d'oeuvres, and circulated. Phoenicia spotted a few society acquaintances, and went over to chat with them, all the while employing the small devices secreted in her sequined purse.

Ace also circulated. He went across the big room to joke with the bartender, then ambled back, circling around the tables. Everywhere he went his electronic surveillance continued. He scanned the ornate sculptured plaster ceiling for unnecessary wiring, and found none. He scanned the floor for the same, with similar results.

They eventually took a turn on the dance floor, which gave them a chance to check out the huge, glittery chandelier and the central flooring.

"Fooey," said the girl in disappointed tones. "This place is clean as a whistle!"

Ace smiled blandly, as if accepting a witty compliment. "Sonics show no sliding panels or concealed hiding places behind the walls," he muttered. "And even the basement is clean, just a stone-walled wine cellar and the usual waiter's toilet."

"If this place is rigged as a trap for Zarkon, you could fool me," the girl griped.

Then she glanced at the small diamond-studded watch she wore on one slim, tanned wrist.

"Time to report to headquarters," she said.

"I'll do it," Ace volunteered. "Phones are up front, by the hatcheck room. It'll give me a chance to check the booths out."

They returned to their table and he drew out the chair for Fooey. She seated herself and became busily occupied with finishing her third drink.

The aviator strolled out into the front of the club, exchanged a few words with the maitre d' and chose a phone booth at random. His devices showed nothing unusual in the walls or partitions.

It had occurred to Ace that Zarkon might be lured into a specially prepared telephone booth, on the pretext that a call had come for him, then somehow gassed or dropped, booth and all, elevator-like, into a basement filled with thugs.

To his disappointment, his instruments showed nothing wrong with the phone booths at all.

He dialed headquarters and spoke briefly with Zarkon.

"Chief? Ace. Fooey and I have checked the Golden Apple out thoroughly, and come up with nothing!"

"Nothing?" inquired the voice at the other end.

"Less than nothing," confided Ace. "The joint is clean as a hound-dog's tooth from basement to roof . . . if these fancy gadgets work as well as they're supposed to."

"They do," said Zarkon briefly.

"Okay, then I guess the coast is clear. Seems like no tricky gadgets or rough stuff are in their plans."

"You may leave now," ordered Zarkon, "but park around the corner and wait for a signal. I shall arrive shortly, on time for my appointment with Lucifer. . . ."

"You still mean to go through with it, Chief?" inquired the young aviator. There was a note of strain and anxiety in his voice.

"Yes, but you need not worry about me," said Zarkon gently. "I know what I am doing."

"I hope so," remarked Ace, a bit doubtfully. Like the others, he felt sure that Zarkon would not hesitate to sacrifice himself, if the lives of his friends were endangered. And he heartily disapproved of the sentiment, although he would have done the identical thing himself, under similar circumstances, and without a moment's hesitation.

"On second thought, Ace, you and Phoenicia return at once to headquarters," commanded the Omega Man. And with that, he rang off.

Harrigan ambled back to their table and passed along their orders to his blond companion. She was clearly as disgruntled as he was at being summoned back to base.

"Dang it, I wanted to stick around for the fun!" Phoenicia Mulligan lamented.

"So did I," commented Ace Harrigan.

But orders were orders. They paid their check, added a lavish tip, and left.

While waiting for their car to be driven around to the front, they observed another of Omega's vehicles pulling up in front. In marked contrast to the sleek, velvety-black Supra limousine, it was a battered and worn-out-looking Yellow Cab. Ace grinned faintly, recognizing the cab from earlier adventures: It was as armor-plated as a tank, and it would have taken a platoon of artillery to have stopped it, once it got rolling.

Zarkon stepped out, in modishly stylish evening clothes. He exchanged a brief, friendly nod with Ace and Phoenicia Mulligan, and strolled in with the casual stride of a man out for an evening's pleasure on the town, and certainly not like a man perhaps on his way to his own execution.

They got into their car and followed the Yellow Cab back to their West Side headquarters. Nick Naldini, disguised under a red bandanna scarf and a greasy hack driver's cap, had driven Zarkon to the nightclub.

"What say we disobey for once, and sneak back?" Fooey Mulligan suggested slyly. "If nothing happens, the Chief need never know. If trouble hits, we'll be on the spot."

Ace was very tempted. But, reluctantly, he shook his head. Orders were orders: If people went haring off on their own all the time, no one could be counted on to be where he was needed.

He said as much to Fooey, apologetically.

She shrugged resignedly.

Ace looked gloomy. He wondered if he had just seen Zarkon for the last time in this life. . . .

CHAPTER 21

The Message

Zarkon entered the Golden Apple and was escorted to the table he had reserved for himself earlier. It was situated against a wall, where he could sit facing the room and within clear view of the entrance.

This particular side of the building was solid brick, and beyond it was only the street, so Zarkon could feel reasonably certain no hidden panel existed through which Lucifer might strike at him.

The Man of Mystery ordered a cocktail and relaxed, ignoring the curious faces turned toward him and the lull in the omnipresent buzz of conversation which had fallen upon his entrance into the room. Most of the citizens of Knickerbocker City had, of course, heard the challenge the Earth-Shaker had hurled at him, and more than a few of the Golden Apple's patrons were there to watch Zarkon and to witness what was to happen.

More than a few of these were newspaper reporters and television newscasters. No one approached the Prince as he sat, idly toying with his cocktail, and the eyes turned his way were politely covert and not staring. They wished to give him as much privacy as they could, obviously. Zarkon felt appreciative of their thoughtfulness.

The Man from Tomorrow had not left it up to Ace Harrigan and Phoenicia Mulligan alone to check out the nightclub. He had secretly investigated the building himself from the adjoining rooftops with sensitive, long-range devices. And in a brief tour of the sewer tunnel that ran under the basement, he had also explored.

The results of his examination were identical with those Ace Harrigan and Phoenicia Mulligan had found.

Which is to say . . . *nothing*.

The attack, if attack there would be, then, would come even less obviously than he had previously expected. He glanced down at the frosted goblet he was twirling absently between his fingers, whose chilled contents he had not yet sampled.

Zarkon seldom drank alcohol in any form, although he had no moral or medical arguments for refraining. In fact, he occasionally drank a good vintage wine with one of Chandra Lal's splendid dinners.

At the moment, he had two reasons for not sampling his drink. Not only did he wish to keep his head clear and his reflexes swift, but if Lucifer was not going to strike at him through some hidden mechanism, he could only do so through a foreign substance introduced into food or drink or, possibly, the air itself.

Therefore, if he declined to eat or drink anything, he was relatively safe.

And as a precaution against narcotic or anaesthetizing gas in the air, the Prince wore small tubes clipped inside his nostrils and not easily visible. These were primed with chemicals that filtered such foreign substances from the air he breathed.

For the moment, he could think of no other precautions to be taken.

So he sat back, relaxed yet alert, and enjoyed the floor show and the fine orchestra.

It was going to be a long night.

Just *how* long, in fact, he could not have guessed. . . .

The police commissioner and Mayor Phineas T. Bulver were closeted together at that very moment, arguing bitterly. That is, the commissioner was doing the arguing, while His Honor was keeping silent.

"You must know, Your Honor, what foolishness this is," the commissioner was saying. "If Zarkon is whisked away—or if this madman demolishes the Omega headquarters building—public fears will run rampant. One of the greatest crime fighters of this century will have displayed his total inability to stop one crook. There will be a panic, I warn you, and perhaps even riots in the streets of the city! You should never have yielded to Zarkon on this crazy scheme of walking alone into a deathtrap—I could have filled the nightclub wall to wall with plainclothes detectives—"

"Billy," snapped the Mayor unperturbed, "this Zarkon feller is the real goods. He ain't gonna let this Earth-Shaker or his goons get away with anything, mark my words. Didn't two o' his boys prevent the third bank from bein' destroyed? Well, I trust this prince feller, and I'll go along with his plans—whatever they is, I mean."

"That's exactly what I mean," snapped William Richard "Wild Bill" Prescott, the police commissioner. "What *are* his plans? You don't know and I don't know—"

"And I don't care, dagnabit!"

"But—"

"Stop fumin' like a blocked chimney, Billy; cool off!" advised Phineas T. Bulver. "Zarkon's no fool. If he's goin' in alone and unarmed, he must have a shrewd plan up his sleeve. And he also ain't no saint, either. He's sure not gonna sacrifice himself t' save—"

"The men who follow him, his closest friends and associates?" demanded Wild Bill Prescott sarcastically.

Bulver flushed and mopped his streaming brow. "No, dagnabit, a *buildin'*. He can move out ever' livin' soul from his headquarters. That way, if the Earth-Shaker hits, his men will be safe and only a hunka real estate will suffer. Dagnabit, Billy, I'll *give* him a whole new buildin' if that happens. City repossesses more empty, abandoned buildings in a year nor you could shake a stick at. Nossirree: Leave him be."

Prescott subsided, inwardly seething. The muscles in his lean jaw tightened as he bit down so savagely upon the stem of his battered old briar pipe that it almost snapped in two.

But he knew better than to argue further with Phineas T. Bulver. The fat, waddling little Mayor, with his gift for rich invective and startling candor, might be a comic figure of fun to many, but not to

Wild Bill. He knew just how concerned and dedicated a public servant the Mayor was, and what an honest, sincere man.

But he had taken certain precautions, after all, which he had not confessed to His Honor. Police snipers with night glasses were perched on nearby rooftops, covering every entrance and exit. Unmarked cars, crammed with plainclothes officers, heavily armed, were parked about the vicinity, ready at an instant's notice to block streets and alley mouths.

If Lucifer killed or tried to carry off Prince Zarkon, Wild Bill Prescott intended to stop him. Zarkon might have persuaded the Mayor of Knickerbocker City into going along with his seemingly suicidal plan, but the law was the law.

And the police commissioner was not going to knowingly be an accomplice to murder or kidnapping.

Time passed with agonizing slowness, the second hand of Zarkon's watch seemed to crawl, as always is the case when you are waiting for something to happen. But the bronze-faced man with the pewter-gray hair showed no visible strain or nervousness. He did not tap on the tabletop with his fingertips, or fidget. He seemed as calm and untroubled as any other gentleman out for an evening's entertainment.

Inwardly, Zarkon was becoming puzzled at Lucifer's failing to strike on time. Was the wily mastermind of crime frustrated from striking by the precautions he and his men had taken in so thoroughly checking out the club? Or had the police, after all, and against the Mayor's orders, cordoned off all approaches to the Golden Apple?

Phineas T. Bulver had assured the Prince that no one would interfere with his decision to venture alone and unarmed into the fashionable nightclub. But public pressure can bring to bear, even on a Mayor, terrific force. Perhaps Bulver had given way and let Commissioner Prescott have his way.

Zarkon frowned thoughtfully. He felt inwardly certain that this was not the case. He decided that Lucifer's lateness was simple precaution: The Napoleon of Crime was making triply certain that he, himself, was not stepping into the open jaws of a trap.

Or was Lucifer waiting for Zarkon to take a drink from the cocktail he held in his hand?

Zarkon lifted the goblet to his lips, smelled the aroma of the beverage, even touched the surface of the liquid it contained with the tip of his tongue.

His senses of smell and of taste had been honed to a keenness seldom found in ordinary men, by special exercises. But he could neither smell nor taste anything suspicious or out-of-the-way in the beverage, but that did not mean nothing was there. There are drugs and poisons, he knew, too subtle or too odorless and tasteless for their presence to be discovered so easily.

Zarkon had spent years immunizing himself against as many of the known drugs and poisons as possible. He felt confident that his superb physique could throw off the effects of any harmful agent in the cocktail far more swiftly than could the finest athlete.

But still he did not sample the drink. Still he waited, relaxed yet poised and ready, for some clue or sign, some message or signal from Lucifer.

Even his stainless-steel nerves were beginning to tauten under the terrific strain of waiting. Even his bottomless patience was beginning to run out, as the seconds and the minutes ticked slowly but inexorably past.

It was a proof of his amazing degree of self-control, then, that he neither jumped nor visibly flinched when suddenly one of the waiters materialized at his elbow.

"A message for you on the telephone outside in the lobby, sir," said the waiter.

"Thank you." Zarkon smiled quietly, getting to his feet.

CHAPTER 22

The Key to the Mystery

Zarkon entered the lobby and went into the telephone booth the waiter indicated. He shut the door behind him and took a seat. Picking up the receiver he spoke into it. "This is Zarkon," he said quietly.

The voice at the other end was excited. "Highness, this is Wilcoxon at the lab. Among the burnt papers from the warehouse we have been piecing together and photographing in infrared is what seems to be the one you are looking for."

Zarkon relaxed. He had expected that the call was from Lucifer; instead, it was good news. "Are you absolutely certain?" he asked tensely.

"Sir, I am almost positive: a geological contour map of the harbor, the river, and the island upon which Knickerbocker City is built," replied the voice at the other end.

"Are the fault lines shown on the map?" he inquired.

The voice sounded almost hysterical in its excitement. "Absolutely! And the 'flaws,' too, in exquisite detail. And every measurement is precisely calibrated on a side strip, with a grid overlaying the—"

But Zarkon had heard enough. He cut Wilcoxon off abruptly. "I must have that photograph as soon as possible," he said urgently. "Bring it to me at once—commandeer one of the police traffic-control helicopters. You can land and pick me up in the street outside the Golden Apple, on Fourteenth Street. Use my emergency authorization number, C11924. With that number, you can override even a divisional commander of—"

"I have already anticipated the urgency of the matter, sir," acknowledged Wilcoxon. "I have a 'copter standing by outside the laboratory at this moment."

Zarkon glanced at his watch. His face tightened grimly, and a bleak light flashed in his magnetic black eyes.

It was eleven minutes after twelve midnight.

Forty-nine minutes from now, the Earth-Shaker would destroy Omega headquarters.

"Bring the map to me at once," he said urgently. "Every minute counts! And tell your pilot to be prepared to pick me up and take me to Omega Island."

"I'm on my way, sir," promised the excited technician.

Zarkon hung up and dialed Omega headquarters.

Ace Harrigan happened to answer the phone. "Yes, Chief?"

"Get everyone out of headquarters," rapped Zarkon swiftly. "Meet me at the island just as soon as possible. If you arrive there before me, get the *Captain Nemo* ready for immediate use."

"Right," said the aviator crisply. "Listen, Chief, what about the kid? He's still hanging around the place—"

"The Weston boy? Bring him with you. I don't want anyone at all left in the building . . . we have, at most, three quarters of an hour before Lucifer strikes."

"What about the equipment, the files, the lab stuff?" asked Ace Harrigan.

"Bring the Belshazzar pistols," said Zarkon. "Leave all the rest. Everything else can be replaced, except a single human life. *Move!*"

He hung up, tossed a bill at the hovering waiter, and left the nightclub. On the sidewalk, loitering near a newsstand, the Prince saw a plainclothes detective whom he recognized, and went up to him. The fellow flushed guiltily, and Zarkon did not need to be the master psychologist that he was in order to realize that Commissioner Prescott had planted some plainclothes cops around the Golden Apple for his protection.

"Please clear the street in front of the club at once," he said. "A police helicopter will be landing in minutes."

The cop jumped into action, tootling his whistle, summoning others from the crowd of onlookers.

Zarkon looked at the sky, then down at his watch again, and his jaw tightened with helpless impatience.

Every minute that went by brought Omega headquarters closer to utter and complete destruction.

And the minutes were ticking by, one by one. . . .

As it happened, the police helicopter did not actually land on the street pavement, but hovered, lowering a rope ladder with which to climb into the canopy.

The big, noisy, blue-and-white chopper alarmed the late-night crowd which drifted from bar to bar and restaurant to restaurant. But the plainclothes cop had effectively closed off the Golden Apple's block, and Zarkon caught the rungs and swung himself up; clinging to the struts, he clambered into the plastic bubble, where Wilcoxon sat next to the police pilot.

The lab scientist was a skinny, rabbity, nervous and heavily-bespectacled little man, swallowing anxiously. In one hand he clutched a large piece of photographic paper.

They didn't even wait long enough for Prince Zarkon to take a seat before whirling up into the sky and arrowing across the city toward the riverfront.

By the light of a penlight and with the use of a magnifying glass he always carried, Zarkon pored over the photograph handed to him by the lab technician.

With painstaking care, the lab scientists had pieced together fragments of burned paper, held under glass, then had photographed the entire document by the use of infrared light, which made the writing on the paper visible.

"Good work," he murmured in an aside to Wilcoxon, who flushed with pleasure at the brief words of praise.

The photograph showed exactly what Zarkon had expected it to show. The relief map of the riverbed and of the island on which

Knickerbocker City was built was exquisitely detailed, and by the grid references he could locate Omega headquarters with perfect precision.

It was indeed on a "flaw."

"Sir?" asked Wilcoxon tentatively. "Does the map show you the information you wanted?"

Zarkon nodded. "Yes; everything that I wished to know is here," he said.

He glanced down. They were soaring over the docks now, and the dark waters of the Henry Hudson River stretched beyond, all the way to the Jersey cliffs.

When they were over the water, he peered down. A low-slung, powerful speedboat was cutting the waves, its prow slicing the black water into white foam like a knife blade going through ice cream.

With his pocket binoculars, adjusted to night vision, he studied the people aboard the small, speedy craft. There was no mistaking Fooey Mulligan's blond hair flying on the breeze, or Doc Jenkins' clumsy hugeness.

He smiled briefly: It looked as if he in the chopper and the Omega men in the boat would arrive at the small private island in the middle of the river, where Zarkon kept most of his small fleet of sea- and aircraft, at just about the same time.

CHAPTER 23

Omega Attacks!

As soon as Ace Harrigan hung up the phone, the Omega men sprang into action. While Scorchy ran around collecting everyone on the premises, Menlo Parker scuttled into the equipment lockers to get the Belshazzar pistols which the Chief had requested. These were odd-looking hand weapons with bell-shaped muzzles, resembling no other automatics ever devised. They had been invented by Gabriel Wilde, one of Zarkon's fellow members of the Cobalt Club.

They were generally not available, and, in fact, outside of Wilde's own prototype, these were the only firearms of this exclusive model in the world. Never covered by patent, they were almost unknown.

But Zarkon had a very special reason for requesting that they be brought along, in lieu of the usual weapons carried by his five lieutenants, as will eventually be shown.

Nick, Menlo, Doc, Scorchy, Ace, Fooey Mulligan, Chandra Lal and little Joey Weston were mustered for the departure. The tall, dignified Rajput had been concocting an exquisite soufflé for a midnight snack, but he instantly abandoned his confection at Ace's word, pausing only to turn off the gas and to cast a brief, rueful glance at the oven as he sacrificed a soufflé that would have brought an admiring smile to the lips of Oscar of the Waldorf.

"Everybody out—right now! Chief's orders!" snapped the handsome aviator, thumbing the button that would summon an elevator to take them all to the basement garage.

Menlo Parker was hopping agonizedly from one foot to the other. "What about my laser-beam cyclotron?" he squeaked in anguished tones. "My scientific files and records? The *library?* My working model of the radio-ionic gun? My current experiments—?"

"Chief says everything can be replaced in time, except a single human life," Harrigan said curtly. "C'mon!"

They piled into the elevator, Menlo groaning in anguish, and dropped like lead plummets to the basement, where Zarkon parked his fleet of cars. But they were not taking a car to Omega Island, of course.

They ran across the block-long concrete floor and found the speedboat facing the water doors, and clambered aboard. Chandra Lal took little Joey Weston under his care.

The doors burst open and the speedboat flew down a chute to hit the waves with a belly smack you could have heard—or *felt*—half a block away.

Ace wrestled the wheel, and the motor awoke with a throaty roar. The boat shot out into the current, breasted the waves with sickening force, then steadied itself and clove the dark, cold waters, heading to midriver, where the mysterious island fortress of Omega rose, all but unknown to the majority of the citizens of Knickerbocker City.

The night was cold and clear, the wind brisk. They shivered in the salty spray as the speedboat cut through the dark waters.

Looking up, they spied a helicopter soaring overhead. They did not at once realize that Zarkon himself was in the police chopper, although they might have guessed.

"What's this-here island?" whispered Joey Weston to the majestic Rajput servant.

"The place where the *sahibs* keep moored the various vehicles they employ in the destruction of evil," replied the Hindu in measured and sonorous tones.

"What kinda vehicles?" the boy asked excitedly. The past day and night had been, for the newsboy, an adventure more exciting and colorful than any he could have ever dreamed, and he was bursting with questions.

In solemn tones, Chandra Lal enunciated the various dirigibles, jet- and rocket-planes, 'copters and seagoing vessels the Omega men had at their command, including the nuclear yacht, *Brian Boru,* which had yet, to his knowledge and experience, to be used.

Among these was, of course, the submarine *Captain Nemo.*

"Gollywhoppers! A submarine—!" breathed Joey Weston in ecstasy.

"Even so, little *sahib,*" said Chandra Lal.

They raced across the black waters in record time. The shaggy, forest-grown shores of Omega Island rose before them, a dark bulk rising out of the waves. The river was not very wide at this point, and the voyage took only seconds, since Ace, cognizant of the approaching danger point in time, was pushing the racy craft to its limit.

All the while, the police helicopter kept pace with them from above.

The speedboat pulled up at the covered dock with a flourish and a showering spray of shattered water. Ace Harrigan idled the engine, maneuvering the craft into place while Scorchy Muldoon clambered to the rear to make her lines secure.

Doc Jenkins, Menlo Parker and Nick Naldini jumped out onto the pier and pelted across the tarmac to the long, armored shed where the private submarine rode at anchor.

Phoenicia Mulligan, Scorchy Muldoon, Chandra Lal and the little newsboy, Joey Weston, waited behind for Zarkon's helicopter to land. Ace came trotting up from the boat to join them.

Zarkon ordered the chopper to hover, spun the door seal, and swung out to drop lightly to the pavement. He waved a hasty farewell as the chopper rose on whirring vanes, circled the small island once, and floated off in the direction of the city, whose skyscrapers marched like a row of stone titans on the horizon.

Scorchy had lugged along the special pistols Zarkon had asked for. He tossed one to his Chief; then they all sprinted in the direction of the long shed.

Phoenicia Mulligan and Joey Weston were thrilled by the rarity of this experience. Omega Island is under the Novenian flag, and has diplomatic immunity for that reason. Few and rare are the visitors allowed on the island.

They entered the shed and found the long, gray, cylinder-shaped craft with its sleekly streamlined conning tower riding at anchor in a troughlike concrete dock. The little newsboy had never seen a submarine before, and the prospect of actually riding in one was exciting in the extreme.

But there was no time now for sight-seeing. They piled aboard, and Ace Harrigan ran to the controls. Menlo and Doc had already begun the warming-up procedures. Nick lingered behind to close and seal the air lock.

"Submerge at once," ordered Zarkon, entering the bridge. He unfolded the photograph which Wilcoxon had given him and placed it on a table whose top resembled the ground-glass screen of a powerful televisor. Illumination flared under the glass, making the infrared photograph crisp and sharply clear in every detail.

They crowded around, staring at it eagerly.

Whatever it meant, they knew that it held the key to the mystery of the Earth-Shaker.

CHAPTER 24

The Captain Nemo *Sails*

With the capable hands of Ace Harrigan at the controls, the *Captain Nemo* woke to roaring life. The atomic submarine left its moorings and glided down the sloping, concrete, troughlike channel into the open water, submerging with barely a ripple to mark its passage from view.

Zarkon told the aviator exactly what to look for. With a touch at the controls, illuminated panels sprang into life, depicting the views from forward and aft, above and below. The submarine sank to the bottom of the river, a morass of slick mud littered with a thousand bits of garbage and debris. It nosed into the main channel and began gliding along the clifflike sides of the underwater canyon.

The sheer stone walls of the island whereupon Knickerbocker City was built rose to one hand; to the other, mud sloped away to the distant ramparts of Jersey.

Zarkon returned to the central control room, where his men and friends eagerly awaited his coming. At his appearance, a hubbub of questions arose.

"What happened in the Golden Apple?" demanded Phoenicia Mulligan.

"Yeah, did Lucifer try t' grab ya?" asked Scorchy Muldoon.

"What's this-here thing on the map table?" inquired Nick Naldini curiously.

Zarkon raised both hands to stem the tide of inquiries. "Please," he smiled. "Everything will now be explained." He pointed to the photographic map pinned to the glass-topped, illuminated table before them.

"This is the one document that was missing from the Z-9 file kept under lock and key all these years in the offices of the Mayor of Knickerbocker City," he said. "How Lucifer learned of its existence, I have no way of guessing. But learn of it he did, and he stole it therefrom, although he left the remainder of the file intact."

"Well, Chief, what the heck *is* it?" inquired Doc Jenkins, peering at it puzzledly.

"A geological relief map of the sea bottom, the harbor and the river, as well as the bedrock on which Knickerbocker City is built," explained Zarkon.

"It is the work of a certain Dr. Alexei Zorka, a brilliant inventive genius and scientist who died in the late nineteen thirties. Zorka discovered that Knickerbocker City is built adjacent to a major fault line, which he named 'the Amsterdam Fault'—"

"Then the city *is* in an earthquake zone, after all!" exclaimed Scorchy Muldoon in amazed tones.

Zarkon nodded somberly. "It is, although very little of this has ever become known, even to the experts. At the time, Zorka tried to blackmail the city government, threatening to trigger the Amsterdam Fault with depth charges planted in such a way as to ruin the metropolis. He was stopped just in time, and the authorities figured it would be wise to rebut his claims by naming him a fraud."

"I s'pose, if it was known the city is in an earthquake zone and on a major fault line, however inactive, real estate values would plunge," murmured Nick Naldini to himself, fingering his lean jaw thoughtfully.

Zarkon nodded. "The map was hidden away, and the newspapers were told that Zorka was a harmless maniac and that his claims as regards the so-called Amsterdam Fault were nothing more than a hoax aimed at bilking the city government out of many millions of dollars," he said.

"If the municipal authorities had not done this," he added, "the city would have faced financial disaster. But one copy of Zorka's secret map of the Amsterdam Fault was preserved, in the name of science. It was kept in the wall safe in the Mayor's office."

"And Lucifer somehow found out about it," murmured Fooey Mulligan.

Zarkon smiled at the blond girl. "Yes; how, we shall probably never know. Perhaps he had met Zorka, or knew him, or talked to him in prison. How Lucifer found out does not really concern us at present; it is merely a background detail which we can fill in later. . . ."

Scorchy was poring over the map.

"Chief, I see the big bold zigzag line down the middle of the river," he said plaintively, "that must be the Fault; but what are these little skinny lines shooting off to the sides, under the island itself?"

"Those are called 'flaws,'" Zarkon explained. "They emerge from the main fault line at right angles. They run into the bedrock of the island, splitting it into segments. If we had a grid map of the city, showing every block, we could lay it over the map and I could pinpoint just where the two banks stood on the flaw lines, the ones that Lucifer destroyed, and the one he had next intended to destroy. Omega headquarters itself rests on another of these flaws, this one here."

He touched a hair-thin line which diverged from the main crack in the earth's crust at a sharp angle. The Omega men shivered at the realization.

"How was anything this important hushed up?" inquired Phoenicia Mulligan.

Zarkon looked at her. "Once the authorities had immobilized Zorka, it was officially given out that he had only been bluffing, hoping to panic the city fathers into paying up a hefty ransom. The local, and minor, earthquakes that he had already caused in order to prove his claim, were explained away as having been caused by buried explosives. To this day, hardly a single human being knows of the very existence of the Amsterdam Fault, and I intend to see that things stay this way, if we are successful in crushing the Earth-Shaker."

"How'd'ja stumble onto all of this, Chief?" asked Menlo Parker curiously.

"It was something that turned up during one of my brief conversations with the investment broker, Rutledge Mann," confessed Prince Zarkon. "He appeared to be puzzled, because not all of the banking institutions threatened by the Earth-Shaker were of the same importance or monetary wealth. He could think of no way to account for the fact that Lucifer was trying to extract ransom money both from first-class establishments, like the Jefferson, and from relatively minor companies, such as the State Fidelity. It sprang into my mind that the villain, whom I had not at that time positively identified as Lucifer, was working with actual fault lines, and could not just threaten any one bank, but only those built over the fault or its flaw lines.

"This led me to a conference with Littlejohn, who knew, or had deduced, the true story of the Amsterdam Fault. He knew where all that remained of Zorka's papers were stored. Only the relief map of the Fault itself was missing, so I knew that Lucifer must have purloined it, and that his threats were very real and not pure bluff."

"Okay, okay," breathed Fooey Mulligan, "but you haven't yet explained exactly how the Earth-Shaker does it. If it isn't buried explosives—and everybody concerned seems to be convinced that it is not—then, *how does he do it?*"

"It's actually quite simple," began Zarkon earnestly. But before he could go on, Ace Harrigan rang him from the controls.

"Chief?" his voice came crackling over the intercom. "Looks like we've found what you were looking for—it's dead ahead! Use Screen One for the enlargement."

They crowded to the instrument-covered wall, where several black-light screens registered a continuous visual survey of the mountainous cliffs which were actually the sides of the island on which Knickerbocker City was built.

They saw a plain of dark mud lapping up against a sheer and soaring wall of stone strata. Midway up, there appeared to be a deep cleft sealed with a steel, valve-like door.

"Is that what you were lookin' for, Chief?" inquired Harrigan.

Zarkon grimly said it was. He consulted the map: That particular cleft, one of the major flaws which branched off from the Fault itself, which was long since inactive and by now buried under fathoms of solid mud, had not changed in any aspect since first the hands of Dr. Alexei Zorka had traced it on this very map, back in 1937.

"Move in and check it out," he ordered crisply.

The *Captain Nemo* slowed its forward progress to a mere crawl, nosing toward the flaw. With electronic surveillance equipment, Ace Harrigan probed the steel valve.

"Seems to be locked with one of those numerical code locks, Chief," he announced after checking his instruments.

Zarkon glanced at his watch, and his lips tightened thinly.

"Use the 'master key,'" he ordered.

Harrigan touched a switch. A radio tightbeam hurled a series of signals against the locked valve. In rapid-fire sequence, the signals repeated every numerical combination possible, within the sequential range of a lock of such design. Faster than you would imagine, the beam ran through tens of thousands of combinations—eventually hitting by chance upon the correct, unlocking signal code.

The huge valve swung open, disclosing a lighted inner section.

"Move in and dock," ordered Zarkon.

Ace Harrigan complied. The submarine glided through the open portal, still underwater, and entered into a vast cavernous space, according to its sonar.

"Surface," ordered Zarkon. And with those words he turned to his lieutenants. "Get ready for action," he said crisply. "And remember this above all else: The only weapons we will be using from here on in, no matter what happens, are Belshazzars!

"Let's go!"

CHAPTER 25

Cavern of Mystery

The *Captain Nemo* entered the tunnel which lay beyond the huge steel doors. Sonar waves went *pinggg* against the sides of the passage as the sleek, cigar-shaped submarine cruised forward cautiously. When the instruments informed Ace Harrigan that the tunnel ended dead ahead, he raised the periscope, and then, on instructions from Prince Zarkon, surfaced.

They were floating in a sort of concrete trough filled to the brim with river water. Above them arched the rugged curve of a huge cavernlike opening in the solid rock.

Beside them, a second submarine floated in its dock. It was a smaller machine, the sort that can most easily carry four men within it at one time.

It bore no markings.

Huge banks of fluorescent tubes lit the cavernous space as bright as day. A cement pier ran all around the trough. Diving suits were suspended on overhead racks; tanks of compressed oxygen were piled nearby, where boxes of tools could be seen scattered about.

Other than this, the place seemed deserted.

Ace Harrigan broke the seal, and the Omega men climbed out with guns drawn. On strict orders from Zarkon, Phoenicia Mulligan, Joey Weston and Chandra Lal remained behind in the submarine. Zarkon had soothed their injured feelings by promising them that their help would be called upon if it was needed.

It never hurt to have a backup force available and on call. Zarkon knew better than to put all of his eggs in one basket, as the saying goes.

The Omega men jumped to the pier and stared around. The place was huge, and it must have cost a fortune to construct this facility in secret. Scorchy's lips puckered in a low, admiring whistle.

"Boy," he breathed to Nick Naldini, "no wonder Lucifer's so hot on sticking the banks for a coupla million smackers—musta cost that much to build this place alone!"

Zarkon spied watertight doors directly ahead, where the pavement met the rugged walls. He headed for them at a run, his Belshazzar drawn and ready.

Time was running out, he grimly knew. It was go for broke by this point, with little or nothing to lose.

Suddenly the door swung open on huge gimbals, with a snaky hiss of compressed air. A bunch of thugs in gray coveralls appeared in the opening. They spotted the Omega operatives bunched together on the pavement and came at them with deadly purpose.

Oddly enough, they bore instead of pistols little weighted Y-shaped batons of smooth, hard wood. The tips of the pronged wands were heavy balls.

Zarkon recognized these peculiar weapons as the *onga* sticks used in certain of the martial arts. And he suppressed a quiet smile, for one of his guesses had just been proved accurate. There was no reason for the men not to be armed with guns, unless. . . .

"Oboyoboyoboy!" burbled Scorchy Muldoon cheerfully, his blue eyes lighting up with excitement. The little prizefighter rubbed his palms together briskly and jumped into the fray. Outside of a bevy of blondes, the feisty Irishman enjoyed nothing so much as a good brawl, and this had all the makings of one of the best to come his way in months.

Zarkon was already among the front rank of the attackers. His oddly shaped pistol was holstered beneath his coat, but his bare hands were out, floating at shoulder level. As he stepped forward to meet the charging thugs, these hands drifted here and there, touching the men lightly, seemingly effortlessly.

Men fell as if poleaxed. Most did not even have a chance to cry out before dropping unconscious to the floor. One or two managed to get out a choked grunt or a startled cry before being felled by those strangely effortless blows.

Aboard the *Captain Nemo*, Miss Phoenicia Mulligan was watching these events enviously through the periscope in the cabin. Her mouth dropped open as she watched Zarkon weave through the gang of crooks, felling them to either side with his bare hands.

"What is he *doing*?" she murmured in exasperation. As it happened, she had never seen the Prince in hand-to-hand combat before, and found the spectacle an astonishing sight.

Chandra Lal put his own eye to the periscope. The dignified Rajput smiled faintly and turned to address the surprised girl.

"It is *ahdti*, of which the *sahib* is a master," he explained in his sonorous voice. "*Ahdti* is one of the martial arts practiced largely in Tibet, *memsahib*. He is one of the very few in this hemisphere to have mastered this difficult and little-known art. . . ."

Fooey wet her lips nervously. The attractive heiress wished most urgently to be out there mixing it up with the thugs herself, as inactivity soon bored her. But she watched Zarkon at work with amazement.

Now the other men jumped into the fray. Scorchy's fists were swinging, and from the expression of sheer pleasure on his pugnacious face, Phoenicia guessed he was having the time of his life. He was knocking men this way and that, grinning happily.

Nick Naldini, beside him, was using jiu-jitsu, and men were literally flying to either side of the lank, long-legged magician. Menlo was slugging away with the barrel of his Belshazzar and had already felled two thugs twice his weight.

Doc Jenkins was the only casualty. He had just thrown three men off the pier when he took the weighted end of one of the *onga* sticks alongside of his head. His eyes went blank and rolled up inside his head; his determined expression became serene and detached, and he sat down suddenly, in several places, like a collapsing lawn chair, and rolled over like one suddenly deciding to take a snooze.

Zarkon was at his side instantly, defending his stunned lieutenant from the attackers. The Prince had by now downed six or seven opponents and was not even breathing hard. The Tibetan martial art he was using demanded great concentration, but very little physical exertion.

Ace Harrigan was wading into the bunch of crooks, grinning and flailing away with hard-balled fists. Like all of Zarkon's men, he enjoyed nothing so thoroughly as a good fight, but unlike the others, he generally found himself stuck behind the wheel of one or another means of transportation, looking on while the other boys had the fun. Now he was heartily enjoying his share of the combat.

Joey Weston, his eyes glued to the other scope, was swinging his small fists in sympathy with the battlers. "Give 'im a right, give 'im a left!" the boy breathed enthusiastically. "A one-two t' the ol' breadbasket! *Attaboy!*"

Glancing at the excited newsboy, Phoenicia Mulligan gave a rueful chuckle. If sheer determination counted for anything, the plucky kid was six foot tall and tipped the scales at two hundred pounds of solid brawn. With guts to match.

Then—

"Watch out!" the boy breathed. "What's happening to 'em! *Look*—"

Fooey pressed her eye to the scope again to see what had alarmed the lad. To her surprise and consternation, she saw Scorchy go down as if struck by a hammer, with no one near enough to have even touched him.

Nick Naldini looked dazed, and folded in the middle, hitting the pavement next.

Menlo soon followed, and then Ace Harrigan went down. They had nearly disposed of their adversaries, when felled themselves by unseen blows, as if they had been attacked by invisible men.

"Gas!" exclaimed Fooey Mulligan. "It must be—*gas!*"

"Then, why isn't Prince Zarkon out like the rest?" inquired the boy. The blond girl shook her head wordlessly, having no answer to that question.

"There, up on the wall," murmured Chandra Lal. They swiveled the periscope in the direction which he had indicated: steel rings, like the outlets of pipes, were visible. Although no vapor seethed about the orifices, it was conceivable that a colorless knockout gas could be pouring from them.

Something had certainly rendered the Omega men temporarily noncombatant.

Only Zarkon seemed resistant to the invisible force. The remaining crooks folded as neatly as had the Omega men, leaving the gray-clad Crime-Crusader the only man left standing. He looked around swiftly, spotted the same outlets Chandra Lal had just noticed, and went over to them. From the ground, the Man from Tomorrow snatched up some packing material, which he began stuffing into the pipes.

This had no immediate effect on the unconscious men.

"Let's go out and help!" urged Phoenicia. "We can't let Zarkon face Lucifer all alone, without the boys to back him up. That would be suicide!"

The majestic Rajput slowly shook his head in the negative. "The gas would get to us as well if we went outside, *memsahib*," he said sternly.

Fooey glanced around the cabin inquiringly. "Any gas masks here?" she demanded.

"I do not know," said Chandra Lal shortly. The Rajput had never before been in the *Captain Nemo* and had no way of knowing what weapons or equipment it might contain.

"How about the diving suits? Surely they got some of those aboard—suppose they had to go out underwater on one of these junkets?"

"We can look, *memsahib*," said the Hindu. He was as eager to help defend his Prince as was the blond girl and the little newsboy.

They began a rapid search that turned up nothing. If there were any diving suits aboard the atomic submarine, they were not out in plain view.

"You mean, we can't do *anything* to help?" wailed Phoenicia Mulligan desperately.

Muscles bunched along the Rajput's lean jaw, but he said nothing.

Lucifer had won this round, it seemed. And the fight might not last into the second.

CHAPTER 26

The Earth-Shaker at Bay

On the concrete dock, Scorchy Muldoon had just downed one of the crooks with a karate blow and was looking around for another thug to tackle, when suddenly a dazed, stupid expression came over his freckled and snub-nosed countenance. The little prizefighter went down all at once, as if poleaxed, although nobody was close enough to where he stood to have touched him.

Nick Naldini was the next to fall. He was just about to tackle a thug armed with one of the forked rods, when the fellow keeled over as if hit by lightning. Nick stared dumbly at the fallen foe, then went down himself, folding in the middle, and hit the dock like a sack full of laundry.

Menlo toppled over next, followed by Ace Harrigan, and then big, roaring Doc Jenkins, who was happily engaged in bashing the heads of two of the crooks together with his heavy hands. The big man fell as a towering oak falls when cut down by lumberjacks.

And it was not only the Omega men who were falling, but Lucifer's gang, too. They went down one by one—the few that were still standing after the pummeling they had received—leaving Zarkon the only one in the cavern still on his feet.

The Prince instantly realized that Lucifer must have flooded the great room with some invisible sleep gas. He also guessed the reason for his own strange immunity to the anaesthetic vapor.

That is, he still wore the chemical filters clipped into his nostrils which he had worn back in the Golden Apple nightclub and had not bothered to remove since.

He easily spotted the valves set into the wall, wherefrom the sleep gas had been injected into the cavern. Snatching up some sacking material from beside the piled diving equipment, Zarkon stuffed the rough cloth into the valves, effectively blocking them.

Then he lugged two of the steel tanks of compressed oxygen over to where his men lay and began reviving them, one by one. Scorchy and Nick were the first to recover from the effects of the gas, and Zarkon assigned to them the job of reviving Ace, Menlo and Doc Jenkins.

Then he headed toward the rear of the huge, cavernous room, where a door gave entrance into the rooms beyond.

Time was still of the essence.

And time was running out. . . .

Aboard the *Captain Nemo* all this while, Miss Phoenicia Mulligan was itching to get into the action. No less eager to partake in the final act of this adventure were Chandra Lal and little Joey Weston.

Fooey Mulligan began rummaging again through the equipment lockers, where the Omega men kept supplies, weapons and instruments they might need on any case. Suddenly the blond girl uttered a triumphant cry.

"Hot dog!" she crowed. "Looky what I found!"

The tall Rajput grinned, white teeth flashing in his swarthy, bearded face. For the heiress had found a set of light, portable gas masks.

The three hastily donned these, and moments later, Chandra Lal, Phoenicia Mulligan and the little newsboy, Joey Weston, climbed out of the conning-tower hatch and joined the Omega men on the dock.

Together, they succeeded in reviving their slumbering comrades, and Menlo found the controls which operated the air blowers, so they were soon able to flush the sleep gas out of the room entirely, enabling them to breathe freely, without the cumbersome masks.

"These ginks are gonna wake up soon," announced Scorchy Muldoon, examining the thugs felled by their own gas. "Mebbe we better tie 'em up—don't want to leave 'em behind to block us from th' sub."

"Let's give that job to Chandra Lal and Fooey and the kid," suggested Nick Naldini. "The rest of us better get goin'. The Chief may need our help."

They agreed that this was a sensible suggestion. Even Scorchy could find nothing to gripe about concerning it, although the little Irishman heartily disliked having to agree with anything the stage magician said or suggested.

Unlimbering their special guns, the Omega men headed for the door at the rear through which their leader had vanished a few minutes before.

They didn't know what to expect, but in their present mood they were just about ready for anything.

"Dang gas gave me a headache," grumbled skinny little Menlo Parker in a peevish tone of voice.

"Yeah, an' I bumped my head when I went down," mourned Doc Jenkins, nursing a goose-egg on his scalp with tender fingers.

"Shoulda been wearin' nose-filters, like the Chief was, I guess," growled Scorchy Muldoon. The quick-witted Irishman had already figured out how Zarkon had contrived to escape from the gas which had felled the rest of their number.

Nick pulled the door open and plunged in. "Here goes nothing!" he said.

Zarkon prowled swiftly through storerooms, dormitories lined with cots, shower stalls and a small but efficient-looking galley. He found no other person during his rapid search: Apparently, all of the men in the subterranean base had charged out to join the fray on the docks.

Except, of course, Lucifer.

And where might the Earth-Shaker be hiding himself?

And where was Ching? Surely, by now, the suave and cunning little Asian would have rejoined his dread master.

Beyond an inner door, he found the answer to both of these questions . . .

A wall of transparent plexiglass blocked off the rear of the cavern. There, at a huge control console, sat the Earth-Shaker himself, making intricate adjustments on the dials and switches arrayed about him.

Lucifer was still partially swathed in the mummy-like bandages, and still sat in the steel wheelchair.

Behind him, in a long white laboratory coat, the Chinese stood, checking figures on a clipboard.

Behind Lucifer's chair stood an immense black, bare to the waist, displaying an impressively muscled torso. Zarkon recognized the giant Nubian. Originally, Lucifer had had two such black bodyguards, Mongo and Simba. Simba had been killed at the conclusion of that earlier adventure on Mount Shasta, and now only Mongo was left.

Beyond the three men and the control console, Zarkon saw the naked rock of the island itself. In particular, he saw a narrow crevice that wound into unguessable distances. He knew that this was the "flaw" which branched out from the Amsterdam Fault.

Fastened to the sides of the crack in the bedrock of the island were huge, intricate machines. One glance at them and Zarkon's guesses as to the secret of the Earth-Shaker were confirmed.

They were sonic amplifiers.

Lucifer looked up as Zarkon entered the room, and gave a gloating, cold smile.

"You are a remarkably hard man to kill, Prince Zarkon," he said, his words being conveyed to Zarkon by an overhead microphone.

Zarkon said nothing.

Lucifer laid his hand on a red lever and raised the other hand in a gesture of warning. "Only seconds remain before I shall destroy Omega headquarters," he announced. "And you cannot stop me, for all your cleverness and your courage!"

Zarkon pointed the pistol at the Earth-Shaker. "Step away from those controls," he commanded grimly.

The other laughed. "Your knowledge of science is one for which I have the highest possible respect," said Lucifer. "Therefore, I am certain that you have recognized at a glance the nature and purpose of the machinery behind me: a system of linked sonic amplifiers, which conduct sound waves throughout the length of the flaw, triggering an earthquake."

"I know," Zarkon said.

"Then, you understand the reason for this transparent wall of plastic which separates us, and why I am using a throat microphone," continued Lucifer. "The slightest sound will be amplified by these mechanisms, triggering the very earthquake you have come here to prevent."

Zarkon said nothing, his face like stone. But the muzzle of the pistol did not waver. It was aimed directly at Lucifer's heart.

"*You dare not fire that gun!*" The triumph in Lucifer's voice was audible.

And Zarkon knew that they were at an impasse.

CHAPTER 27

The Belshazzar Pistol

For a long moment, they remained in a motionless tableau. Zarkon held his pistol unwaveringly, its muzzle fixed on Lucifer's heart, while the Earth-Shaker sat behind the control console, grasping the red lever in one bandaged hand.

Ching and Mongo stood like statues, waiting for the next move. The little Oriental, his bald brows glistening with beaded perspiration, seemed to be holding his breath.

"So we are at a stalemate, you and I," observed the Earth-Shaker. "My pawn, as it were, blocks your queen!"

"So it would seem," said the Man from Tomorrow noncommittally.

"Already, the sonic amplifiers are warmed up. I was just about to activate the sound-wave projector when you burst in with your rude and untimely interruption," Lucifer said. He smiled thinly. "But now, I hold my hand! If you must fire your revolver, my dear Prince, then please do so . . . the amplifiers can pick up and transmit into the rock strata *any* sound, either sonic or subsonic. And it would be a pleasant cause of ironic amusement to me, if your pistol shot, my dear Zarkon, should cause the very earthquake you wish so desperately to avert. Poetic justice, you might call it . . . but the destruction of Omega headquarters would then be the work of your own hand, not of mine."

Zarkon said nothing, and his face was as expressionless as a piece of carved marble.

Lucifer continued, an inexorable logic underscoring his every word. "Lay down your pistol and elevate your hands, and I will send Mongo out to make you my prisoner—no; say, rather, my guest. For I have long wished that we could work together for the salvation of mankind: Together we could build a new civilization that. . . ."

His words trailed away, for the Master of Mysteries shook his head with stern finality.

"Never," said Zarkon quietly. "Instead, let me suggest a more viable alternative."

"Do so, then," said Lucifer equably. "We have all the time in the world at our disposal."

"You cannot escape," Zarkon pointed out reasonably, "for my men have blocked your escape route. Your own confederates were rendered unconscious by the sleep gas with which you flooded the cavern, and by now, since my own men are back on their feet, your people have doubtless been disarmed and are bound. Your submarine is in my hands and your way to the riverbed is blocked by the presence of my own agents."

"Perhaps," purred Lucifer silkily. Zarkon pressed on, buying time for his men to join him.

"You must know that you have nothing at all to gain by triggering an earthquake now," he said. "All of my people are safely out and the headquarters building is deserted. You will neither destroy my organization nor greatly hamper my effectiveness in fighting crime, by destroying Omega. Nor will your earthquake prevent me from making you my prisoner," added Zarkon.

"Perhaps so," drawled Lucifer. He seemed to be enjoying himself hugely.

"Therefore, I will make this proposal to you now," said Zarkon. His voice was clear, his tone forceful, even commanding. He had long studied the art of rhetoric and knew how to project emotion, how to virtually mesmerize others through speech alone. Now he exerted his skill in this rare art to the fullest. "I entreat you to surrender to me now, you and your accomplices," Zarkon urged. "I have no wish to take your life nor theirs. But if I must fire the gun, fire it

I shall. Blood will be shed and lives may be lost. I would greatly prefer that this solution to our impasse be not required."

"I can agree with those sentiments," admitted Lucifer, smiling slightly.

"Surrender, then, and if you do so openly, I will personally guarantee that you and your two confederates will have a fair and impartial trial. You have little to fear from the justice of the courts, after all—two buildings were destroyed, but few lives were lost. The destruction of property is a serious offense, true, as are threats of extortion. But you could not have hoped to—"

Lucifer shook his head, smiling. "You may save your breath, Prince Zarkon," he said. "I will not surrender—but if you surrender to me now, and lay down your gun, I will spare Knickerbocker City another earthquake, and Omega headquarters will remain standing."

Zarkon took a deep breath.

And fired the pistol.

The explosion of a gunshot in that enclosed space should have been shockingly loud, awakening a host of booming echoes which would have been picked up by the sensitive ears of the sonic amplifiers and transmuted into seismic shock waves.

Instead, when Zarkon fired the peculiar-looking pistol he held directly at Lucifer's heart, the gun made only a faint sound, like a hoarse sigh.

It penetrated the transparent shield.

Had the shield been built of plate glass, it would have shattered with a devastating crash of jangling shards. But plexiglass does not shatter; it splinters and sometimes pulverizes. Therefore, a web of cracks sped through the glassy stuff, and a bullet-sized hole appeared in the center of the web, but no jangling noise accompanied the event.

Lucifer sagged back in his wheelchair, clutching at his bandaged breast, where a red stain appeared above the heart. The mastermind of crime slumped forward even as Zarkon sprang to the splintered shield, taking aim a second time.

Ching and the giant Nubian, Mongo, hastily quitted the control chamber, wheeling the slumped body of their master before them. They vanished into a doorway Zarkon had not noticed.

The Man of the Future was busily prying out sections of splintered plexiglass from the shield frame when his men came bursting through the door, erupting on the scene with drawn guns.

With brief words, Zarkon apprised them of the events which had just occurred. Menlo stared at the machinery curiously.

"Sonic amplifiers—of course!" the wizened savant breathed. "How ingenious!"

"What does it mean?" inquired Ace Harrigan.

The little scientist explained briefly. "We knew the earthquakes couldn't have been caused by explosive charges, because if they had, the seismograph readings would have recorded the biggest vibration at the beginning, then leveled off as the shock waves diminished," Menlo said. "Instead, the tremors grew and built toward a climax from a slow start, just as natural quakes do."

"And—?"

Menlo flapped a hand at the machines. "Subsonics are by definition inaudible," he explained, "but they are vibrations. The amplifiers make them more intense; fed into the crystalline structure of the bedrock beneath Knickerbocker City, they would grow and grow, resulting in a tremor whose seismograph readings would be identical with those in an ordinary earthquake."

Ace turned to Zarkon, who was shutting down the controls. "You guessed all of this, eh, Chief?" he inquired.

The Nemesis of Evil nodded.

"That's why you wanted us armed with Belshazzars," Nick Naldini guessed. "They wouldn't make any noise for the amplifiers to pick up and transmit!"

Zarkon acknowledged that this was so.

"But what the heck *are* Belshazzars!" hotly demanded Miss Phoenicia Mulligan, who had come into the room by this time and was sore that she had missed the final showdown with Lucifer and Ching.

Zarkon showed her the pistol he had fired at the Earth-Shaker. It was oddly designed, with a flaring, bell-shaped muzzle such as on no other firearm the blond heiress had ever seen before.

"The Belshazzar pistol has the most powerful and effective silencer ever devised," Zarkon declared. "The guns are not in general use and their design is still secret. They were invented by one of my colleagues in the Cobalt Club, an adventure-minded socialite named Gabriel Wilde. At my request, some years ago, he provided me with samples of the gun."

"Well . . . they certainly came in handy this time!" the girl murmured. Zarkon solemnly agreed.

CHAPTER 28

The Earth-Shaker Vanishes

It did not take Prince Zarkon and Menlo Parker very long to figure out the control console, and they shut it down with promptness. They even severed the power connection, for the sake of ensuring safety.

While this was being done, Nick and Scorchy were trying to open the hidden door through which Ching and Mongo had carried off the body of their master. It was painted to look like stone but was actually built out of steel, and they were having plenty of trouble with it. Even a crowbar found in a tool locker failed to pry the stubborn metal loose.

Zarkon and Menlo Parker gingerly dismantled the sonic amplifiers so that they could not, either by accident or by some remote-control device, be triggered. Having saved Omega headquarters from destruction by earthquake, they did not wish to risk it further.

And once the machines had been rendered completely harmless, Zarkon removed from their innards several key components not easily replaced. These he crushed underfoot, thus ensuring that the earthquake-causing devices could never again be used, either by Lucifer or another criminal, without expensive and extensive repairs.

By this time, the steel door stood open.

"Okay, Chief," puffed Scorchy Muldoon with satisfaction, briskly rubbing his bruised hands together as if sheer muscle power alone had accomplished the trick.

Actually, it had been the sensitive fingers of Nick Naldini which had picked the lock. The ex-vaudeville stage magician, cardsharp, ventriloquist and escape artist had also dabbled in safecracking during his brief venture into a criminal career, before Zarkon had salvaged him from ruin.

"I supplied th' muscles," boasted Muldoon.

The door opened upon a small cubicle, obviously an elevator shaft whose car was driven by compressed air, from the looks of the mechanism. The car was gone and there seemed to be no way to call it back to its starting place.

"Let it go," advised the Lord of the Unknown. "We have drawn Lucifer's fangs, and he is harmless, even if he does somehow manage to survive my bullet. His entire gang is under lock and key, we have control of his submarine, and his earthquake machine has been destroyed. He can do us no further harm at present, nor can his two confederates."

"You don't really think he can live through a scene like that, do you?" demanded Fooey Mulligan incredulously. "Why, you put a shot through his heart!"

Zarkon shrugged, saying nothing. It was not his wont to speak on anything he did not know for certain.

But Menlo Parker had the last word in this case. "That Lucifer has more danged lives than the proverbial cat!" exploded the wizened little man. "Wouldn't put it past him to have figgered a way outa dyin'. . . ."

There was nothing they could add to that. Lucifer had escaped them before, and might well have done so this time. Although how yet remained unexplained. . . .

When they were finished with their work in the inner chamber, the Omega men trooped back into the central cavern, where Chandra Lal stood guard over the captive thugs.

There, Zarkon used the shortwave radio aboard the atomic submarine to place a call to the Knickerbocker City police force. The operator patched his call through to the commissioner, who had been tensely standing by to see what would happen.

Prince Zarkon quietly transmitted a brief message informing Wild Bill Prescott of the destruction of the Earth-Shaker and asking that police boats be standing by off Omega Island to take charge of the prisoners.

They loaded the bound crooks aboard the *Captain Nemo* and shut down the power that supplied the machines in the cavern, so that it would not ever again be used by the forces of evil. Since Lucifer had merely tapped into an underground power line, this was easy enough to accomplish.

"What about the sub, Chief?" inquired Doc Jenkins, cocking one huge thumb at the small vehicle moored at the dock beside their own.

"Scuttle it," said Zarkon tersely.

"Better put the kibosh on that compressed-air elevator, too, Chief, while we're at it," muttered Scorchy Muldoon. "Can't have no other crooks usin' it, right?"

"Good idea, Scorchy," said the Prince. "Menlo, will you see to it?"

"Sure," nodded Menlo Parker, and snatching up a huge socket wrench, he went off to demolish the mechanism.

Ferrying all of the members of Lucifer's gang to the surface, where police boats waited near Omega Island to cart them off to the slammer, took several trips and consumed two hours. But eventually it was finished.

Wild Bill Prescott himself was at hand to observe the end of this adventure. The commissioner wrung Zarkon's hand and swore feelingly.

"I don't know how you managed it, but that was a good job well done, Prince!" he said earnestly.

Zarkon accepted his congratulations with a nod.

"Mayor Bulver wants to know how much we should let the public know about this case," Prescott added.

Zarkon looked thoughtful. "The existence of the Amsterdam Fault was originally hushed up back in 1937, because it was then believed that the information that Knickerbocker City was in an earthquake zone and was, in fact, built on a major fault line would cause a panic and that real estate values would plummet," he observed. "Obviously, no one is going to put up fifty million dollars to build a skyscraper in a city where earthquakes can happen."

"That's straight," murmured Wild Bill Prescott. "What do you advise us to do?"

"The same reasons exist today for concealing the truth from the public," said Zarkon. "It would still panic the public and destroy realty values, plunging Knickerbocker City into economic collapse and civil chaos. I suggest that Mayor Bulver simply let it be bruited about that the Earth-Shaker worked his marvels by means of dynamite charges buried underground. Nobody need ever be the wiser. . . ."

"I'll see that His Honor gets your message, Prince Zarkon," said the police commissioner. "I'm sure that he will agree with you on the importance of concealing the true facts in this case from the citizens and the press."

Since there was nothing left to be done, the Omega men and their friends left the *Captain Nemo* on Omega Island and returned to their headquarters in Knickerbocker City by speedboat.

Morning was already upon them and the east was filled with light by the time they reentered the block-sized building. While Chandra Lal rustled up some grub for the weary and very hungry crime fighters, Phoenicia Mulligan, with the assistance of Ace Harrigan, made cocktails.

Even Zarkon accepted a dry martini, breaking his usual rule. The strain and exertion of the nightlong sequence of adventures had taken their toll even of his remarkable stamina and endurance.

Scorchy smacked his lips over the drink and looked around the big front room appreciatively.

"Th' ol' place sure looks good," he exclaimed fondly. "Good thing we scotched Lucifer's game before he wrecked it; just wouldn't be the same, livin' somewhere else."

They all agreed with him. It looked as though they were out of danger!

"One thing, though, I don't understand," admitted Scorchy.

"And what is that?" inquired Zarkon.

"The third bank, the one ol' Lucifer didn't wreck," said the pint-sized prizefighter. "Figgered it was cuz the blue van was stuck in the warehouse, under the noses of all them cops. But, Chief, *was* the van important to causin' them quakes?"

"That's right, Chief," Doc Jenkins chimed in puzzledly. "Just what role *did* the van play in these shenanigans—and the instrument box Ching carried, and the stopwatch, too?"

"We can only surmise," murmured Zarkon. "Lucifer and Ching had no opportunity to actually test the sonic amplifiers before they hit the first bank: the Jefferson. Ching was on the scene as an eyewitness observer for his master, timing the quake to see that it struck on schedule."

"And the black box, sir?" piped Joey Weston.

Zarkon gave a slight shrug. "Probably only a signaling device," he explained. "So that Ching could advise Lucifer that he was properly stationed."

"Then howcum Lucifer didn't wreck the third bank?" queried Menlo Parker.

"Because we had him cornered in the warehouse, and he had been delayed by his attempt on my life, our conversation, and his escape by means of the bathysphere," said Zarkon. "By the time he was safely away, it was past time for the Berkeley bank to have been destroyed, so he just canceled it. By that time, he had decided to strike next at Omega headquarters, anyway."

Scorchy looked satisfied. All of the mysteries had been resolved.

CHAPTER 29

Lucifer Lives

Quite early the next morning, the telephone rang and rang on one of the private lines inaccessible to the press or public. Scorchy Muldoon came out in his pajamas, yawning and scratching, to answer the phone's insistent ringing.

He snapped wide awake soon enough. "Yessir, Yer Honor, I'll git him right away," he said in respectful tones into the receiver.

Laying down the phone, the little prizefighter ambled off to arouse Zarkon. Miss Phoenicia Mulligan, who had also been awakened by the shrilling of the telephone, appeared from an inner chamber attired in a nightgown whose gauzy transparency made Scorchy's eyes pop.

"Hot dog!" he whistled appreciatively. She glared at him, then burst into barely suppressed giggles.

"What'r'ya laughin' at?" demanded the feisty Irishman suspiciously. Phoenicia pointed at his attire, trying to muffle the squeals of delighted merriment which temporarily made it impossible for her to speak.

Puzzledly, Scorchy glanced down at his pajamas. They were about two sizes too big for him and hung on his trimly built but diminutive frame rather in the manner a collapsed circus tent hangs on its central pole. But that did not seem to be the cause of Phoenicia Mulligan's giggles.

Could it be the color, or perhaps the pattern? Scorchy doubted it: After all, orange and canary stripes, overlaid with magenta and purple polka dots form a tasteful and even eye-appealing combination.

"Dang crazy wimmen!" he grumbled to himself with a shrug, giving the mystery up as insoluble to the purely masculine intelligence.

He reappeared shortly with Prince Zarkon, who nodded a polite greeting to the blond heiress and crossed swiftly to pick up the phone.

"This is Prince Zarkon speaking, Your Honor," he said into the instrument. Then, for a time, he listened without comment, a slight frown creasing his brows.

Nick Naldini and Doc Jenkins ambled into the big room, and little Joey Weston turned up yawning hugely, garbed in another pair of Scorchy Muldoon's notion of appropriate nightwear.

This particular garment was composed of hideously jarring shades of chartreuse, pink, scarlet and flame orange—a combination of colors probably outlawed by the American Society of Optometrists as dangerous to the human eyesight. Fooey burst into another storm of giggles.

After murmuring a few polite words into the phone, Zarkon replaced the instrument in its cradle and turned to those of his comrades-in-arms who had been awakened.

"What is it, Chief?" inquired Doc Jenkins.

"It would appear that Lucifer somehow managed to survive my bullet, even as Menlo guessed he would," Zarkon advised them grimly. "For the Mayor received a message from him this morning—"

Doc opened sleepy eyes, looking thunderstruck. "Jeepers, Chief, you mean that cunning ol' devil is still on the loose?" he inquired anxiously.

Zarkon nodded. "He appears to have gone into hiding, with Ching and the Nubian, Mongo," said the Master of Omega thoughtfully. "But his farewell note warns that we shall face each other again, in the future, and that the long struggle between us is not yet over."

"Danged guy *has* got more lives than a cat!" muttered Nick Naldini in disgusted tones.

"Didja find out where the pressure elevator led to, Chief?" inquired Scorchy Muldoon.

"Yes, Scorchy, the police found it this morning. It opens into a seemingly abandoned warehouse on Water Street, similar to the one which Joey Weston called our attention to," said Zarkon.

"The main difference between the two buildings," Zarkon added, "is that the second building was never set up as more than a very temporary hideout. At least two automobiles were parked in the structure, but nothing else was found on the premises. We may safely assume that Ching and Mongo bore their master out of the elevator and into the cars, and then drove hastily away to some unknown destination. He was wounded, after all, was Lucifer, although not slain by my shot."

"Tough luck, Chief," murmured Doc Jenkins. He knew what a crack shot Zarkon was, and believed the Prince had somehow missed.

Zarkon felt otherwise. "No, Doc, I am not unhappy that I did not kill Lucifer, although it leaves him free once more to prey upon mankind and to attempt to undermine civilization and bring it down to ruin. I would rather not have been responsible for taking another human life, not even that of Lucifer."

The others nodded without comment. They all were very well aware of the scruples their boss had against taking lives, and while most of them did not exactly sympathize with Zarkon's apparent squeamishness—as Scorchy Muldoon would have put it, summing up the consensus of opinion on this topic among the members of Omega, "the only good crook is a dead crook"—none of them was interested in trying to persuade Zarkon to a different point of view.

"Since most of us are up, what about some breakfast?" suggested Zarkon.

As if he had rubbed a magic lamp, the genie appeared right on cue as if materialized out of empty air by the expression of Zarkon's wish. That is to say, Chandra Lal came into the room, impeccably dressed, bowed a silent greeting, and headed at once for the kitchen. Therefrom, in less time than it takes to mention the fact, a succession of appetizing odors and sizzling sounds came to their attention.

Scorchy drew in a lungful of the delicious aroma, sniffing appreciatively.

"Oboyoboyoboy!" he chortled. "Ham an' eggs, fresh biscuits, pancakes and syrup, sausages, buttered toast—the works!"

Miss Phoenicia Mulligan daintily sampled the redolence. "Don't forget hot coffee and orange juice," she remarked.

Scorchy shot her a suspicious glance. "Ya can't smell *orange* juice, gal!" he cracked.

She assumed a disdainful smile but did not refute his words.

But there was, indeed, a frosty carafe of freshly squeezed orange juice, as they soon discovered.

The rest of that long, lazy day the Omega men and their enigmatic master spent in tying up the various loose ends of the adventure.

Wild Bill Prescott phoned to report that most of the crooks seized in the warehouse or in the underwater cavern had crime records as long as his arm and would be safely stashed away behind bars for quite some years to come.

Unhappily, he had bad news to match this morsel of good news. That is, the police had been completely unsuccessful in tracing the whereabouts of Lucifer, Mongo and Ching from the time they left the second warehouse in the two cars. A five-state alarm was out, but in the absence of any description of the vehicles used, it was extremely doubtful if anything would turn up. This, he added, was regretful.

"Yeah, Commish," said Scorchy Muldoon, who had picked up the phone, "but, ona other hand, look at it this way: Lucifer's on the run, injured, lost his whole outfit and secret hideout, and his entire gang's locked up. It'll be a long time before he's back in shape to tackle us or cause trouble again."

"I hope you're right, Muldoon," said Prescott crisply. "Well, inform Zarkon that if there are any further developments in the case, I will contact him as soon as they emerge."

"Righto!" said Scorchy cheerfully, and he hung up the telephone.

Nick Naldini, stretched out lazily on one of the sofas, lifted his head. "Did the cops dismantle the elevator at the warehouse end, like we did at the bottom of the shaft?" he inquired in a lazy drawl.

"Yep," replied the Irishman. "Guess nobody'll be able to use *that* hideout again."

Just then, Menlo Parker appeared with a briefcase clutched in one bony hand, looking for a driver.

"Which one o' you birds wants to drive me down to City Hall?" he inquired, looking directly at Nick Naldini and ignoring the spark of interest that lit up the bright blue eyes of Scorchy Muldoon.

"I do!" chirped Muldoon.

Menlo pretended that he had not heard, but continued looking with meaningful inquiry at Naldini.

"Oh, okay, what the heck," yawned Naldini, lazily climbing to his feet. "What's happened to Ace?"

Ace Harrigan, equally adept behind the wheel of any vehicle yet invented, seemed to be absent. Menlo reported that he had been sent out to Omega Island to make certain the *Captain Nemo* was battened down safe and secure. It might be many months before the atomic submarine was needed again.

"Why can't *I* drive Menlo to City Hall?" demanded Scorchy in injured tones.

"Prob'ly because Menlo actually wants to get there, instead of the hospital or the traffic court," said Fooey Mulligan wickedly.

CHAPTER 30

Back to Normal

On their way down to the basement parking garage where the Omega men kept their vehicles, Nick Naldini addressed a question to the skinny scientist at his side.

"Say, Menlo, I forgot to ask why we're goin' to City Hall," he remarked interrogatively.

Menlo hefted the locked briefcase clasped under one bony arm. "Chief wants me to return File Z-9 to the Mayor for safekeeping," he said. "Also that photographic relief map the police lab put together from the burned fragments we found in Lucifer's files. Never know when somebody might need 'em again."

"S'pose you're right," murmured Naldini, sliding into the front seat of a sporty coupé. "Let's just hope no other crook like Lucifer ever finds out the file exists."

"Yeah, amen to that, brother!" breathed Menlo fervently. "Although, to do any harm, he'd hafta be a scientific genius like Lucifer to even use the information. . . ."

They drove downtown without mishap and were welcomed by Mayor Phineas T. Bulver. The excitable little man was mopping his perspiring brow with a scarlet bandanna when they were ushered into the plush office.

"Good to see you boys again!" said His Honor earnestly, offering them seats.

Menlo handed over the file, while Phineas T. Bulver called his secretary in to receive the documents and conceal them in the secret wall safe.

"How's everything?" inquired the Mayor. "Now that all the excitement's over, I mean."

"Gettin' back to normal, Yer Honor," admitted Menlo Parker. "Every time one of these adventures ends, it's a sorta letdown, though. Then you gotta hang around waitin' for the excitement to start up again. Usually, we don't hafta wait very long. . . ."

"Yup," nodded the Mayor. "I know what you mean. Dagnabit, though, I sure wish yer boss'd let me give you boys the city medal—sure deserve it."

Menlo and Naldini shrugged affably. It was Zarkon's policy not to accept any honors or tokens of appreciation for the results of their crime-fighting activities, although they had been offered in the past just about everything, up to and including the Congressional Medal of Honor.

The city medal to which the Mayor referred was a handsome gold medallion on a rich silk ribbon, the highest honor a citizen of Knickerbocker City could receive from a grateful municipal government.

"Doesn't matter," said Menlo indifferently. In point of fact, he agreed with Zarkon on this point. Medals were useless: The important thing was to have performed a lasting and important service to the community. He said as much to the Mayor.

"I getcher point," nodded Phineas T. Bulver. "But, dagnabit, boys, you deserve *somethin'*—lissen, stick around for a while, an' I'll take you boys out to lunch. On the city, of course!"

And a superb luncheon was enjoyed by all three, just a bit later on.

It came time for Joey Weston to report to his boss, the newspaper distributor, to pick up his papers to sell on the street corner. Scorchy escorted him to the door and said good-bye, giving his red hair an affectionate tousling.

On the way back in, he met Nick Naldini and Menlo Parker, who had just returned from their sumptuous meal with the Mayor.

"Sure gettin' fond of that kid," admitted the Irishman. "Gotta work on th' Chief, see if he'll let us move him in here. Got plenty o' room, and that crummy rooming house he's livin' in now is in a lousy neighborhood."

Menlo looked dubious. "You know how the Chief feels about putting people in a position of danger," he told Scorchy. "Fat chance you got of gettin' him to take in a kid! Chief's got a heart as big as all outdoors, but sometimes he can be hard as nails and cold as ice."

"Think so, do ya?" sniggered Scorchy nastily, but made no further comment on the affair. He happened to know that Zarkon had already arranged through the investment broker, Rutledge Mann, to establish a college trust fund for the orphan newsboy.

When he gets to college age, he can go to any university in the world with the fifty thousand dollars Zarkon had quietly placed in the fund.

He had a feeling he could work on the Chief. He might be tough about some things, Scorchy well knew, but he had soft spots in his armor.

Scorchy came into the big front room just as Ace Harrigan was leaving it. The handsome aviator had just returned from his trip to Omega Island, and now he wore a rueful expression on his face. Since Ace was generally the most cheerful and uncomplaining of them all, this mystified Scorchy. Looking at Fooey Mulligan and Nick Naldini, Muldoon cocked a thumb at the back of the retreating aviator.

"What's eatin' him?" he inquired curiously. "Gotta face on him as long as Nick's legs. . . ."

The vaudevillian grinned nastily. "Ol' Ace just got turned down!" the magician announced with a chuckle. "Asked Fooey here to have dinner with him and go dancin' or something. Turned him down flat as a pancake!"

Scorchy grinned. The good-looking pilot was usually a hotshot with the ladies, and so seldom got a turndown that you could mark the occasion with a biannual holiday. "Guess he figgered that, after the fun you had at the Golden Apple, you were sweet on him, eh, Fooey?" he inquired with a leering grin.

She sniffed and said nothing. Then she left the room.

Nick laughed.

Scorchy gave him a mischievous glance. "Mebbe I better find out if Fooey likes long-legged ginks with phizzes like some cheap road-show Dracula," he quipped.

Naldini flushed indignantly. "She'd probably prefer a sawed-off leprechaun like you!" said the magician scathingly.

Scorchy flushed crimson and balled up his fists. "Why, you phoney cardsharp! Begorra, but I've got half a mind t' trim ya down to size wiv me fists!" he declared hotly.

"You got *that* one right, Short Stuff," snarled Nick Naldini. "I've always thought you only had half a mind, and now you've confirmed my opinion!"

"Why, you—!"

"Why, you—!"

They were really at it a few minutes later, when Prince Zarkon came strolling by. He glanced into the room inquiringly.

Phoenicia Mulligan appeared from another room.

"What is happening in there?" asked Zarkon of the blond heiress.

She shrugged casually. "Oh, nothing at all in particular," said the girl.

Zarkon nodded but said nothing.

Things were back to normal sooner than he had expected.

Forty miles from Knickerbocker City, in a hidden room whose very existence was unknown to the outer world, a huge man swathed in white bandages sat brooding in a steel chair.

Behind him stood the motionless figure of a giant black, staring ahead as emotionlessly as might a statue hewn from ebony.

Before him stood a small, slight Oriental with a bald or shaven pate and thick-lensed spectacles. The two had been conferring.

"With the destruction of the amplifiers and the seizure of the cavern, Master, any further employment of the Amsterdam Fault seems beyond our reach at present. As well, we have lost our only copies of the relief map and would have to attempt to purloin it a second time from the City Hall, which might be risky, even foolish," the Oriental was quietly pointing out.

The huge man nodded somberly. "We shall turn our attention to other matters, for the present," he said in heavy tones. "The next project is barely begun, but will soon be underway. We shall be kept busy for some time procuring the necessary funds for the enterprise and recruiting a proper staff. And we must find a more secure and a more convenient base of operations than these present quarters. All of this will take considerable time."

"Yes, Master," agreed the little man softly.

"In the meanwhile, we must continue with the skin grafts," said his mummy-like master. "When next Prince Zarkon and I come face to face, it will be on my own terms and when I am able to command the fullest use of my faculties, mental and physical. See to it!"

The small man bowed humbly and left the room.

The bandaged man sat brooding in his wheelchair. "The world shall hear from me again," he said into the silence. "And I shall yet bring it to its knees. . . ."

THE END

But Zarkon, Lord of the Unknown,
and the Omega men will return in

HORROR WEARS BLUE